The Adventures of
PENELOPE
AND CECE

The Adventures of
PENELOPE AND CECE

OUT OF THE BLUE

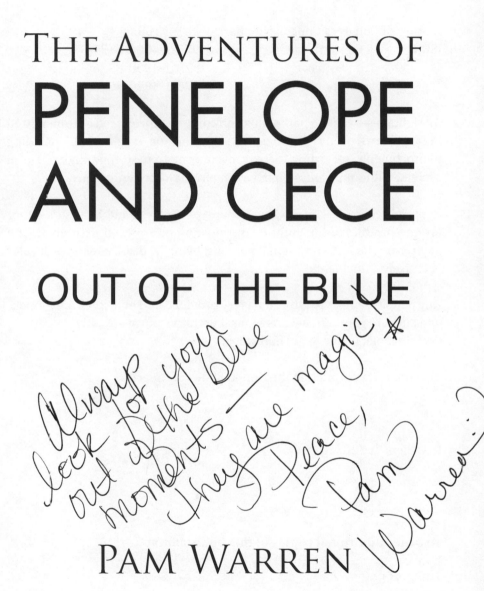

Always look for your out of the blue moments — they are magic! ✦

Peace,
Pam Warren :)

PAM WARREN

To order additional copies of this book, contact:
Xlibris
1-888-795-4274
www.Xlibris.com
Orders@Xlibris.com
551312

For Dad

and

Brad, Terri, Patty, & Peggy + Cindi, & Lolly

Chapter One

CeCe stared at the trees and highway signs of northern Minnesota that were fast-forwarding past her from the window of a Greyhound bus. The trip was long and gave CeCe plenty of time to run through conversations with her mother from the past week. It was all happening so quickly. She still couldn't believe she was meeting her father. And, she had a sister.

The discussions with her mother left CeCe confused, angry, and filled with questions.

Her first reaction had been loud and persistent. "Mom? What? You contacted my father? Why? Where is he? How long have you known? I don't get it, why now? Mom?"

CeCe couldn't understand why her mother had contacted her father and wanted the two of them to build a relationship. Why reconnect now after so many years?

Mae gave explanations such as "I wanted a new start." "I thought I could raise you on my own." "We didn't get along anymore." "I'm sorry. I wish I had done things differently." "He could have found you if he wanted."

All of her mother's excuses seemed weak and didn't make much sense to eleven-year-old CeCe, who had always had questions about her father and never had answers to quench her curiosity. At times, she had hoped that they could one day meet, and he would answer that long list of questions. At other times, she didn't want any contact with him, ever. How could he have abandoned her? Now she was going to have to spend two weeks with him, and that sounded frightening and, quite possibly, unbearable.

CeCe's reaction to the second part of her surprise was quiet.

"I have a sister?" she whispered.

Discovering her father had another daughter meant that CeCe had a sister—a half-sister. She could not have predicted a sibling, and it sent her mind reeling. H o w old was she? She must be younger. Would she like her? Would they like each other? Was she willing to share her father? What if neither of them liked her? What if CeCe didn't like either of them?

It seemed so unfair that someone else, her sister, was being raised by the man who hadn't even contacted his first born daughter in nine years. How could CeCe know that he wouldn't leave her again?

She couldn't think like that much longer because in only a few moments, she would meet them both. She would be face to face with the man who was her father, and she would meet her sister for the first time. There was so much that could go wrong. But what if it all went right?

*   *   *

Penelope hugged her arms and wiggled her feet then swung her head back and forth as if on a pendulum. Time had stopped. Waiting for the bus was hard.

"Mmm, do you think she will be here soon, Dad?" Penelope mumbled while biting on the fresh hangnail framing her thumb.

"Honey, she will be here soon," John replied as his head twisted back and forth, searching for the same answer. "Are you ready for this?" he questioned and took Penelope's hand and squeezed.

Penelope was looking into his blue eyes, and her hand hugged back as she said, "I'm ready." Her stomach was not as confident though. She wanted to stay brave for her dad, whose anxieties became more evident as the important day approached. His long legs pacing, his checking and rechecking of lists, even his straightening of cushions on the couch had become so obsessive that Penelope was trying to decide how to shake some sense back into her father.

"It's coming! Look! It's coming!"

Following Penelope's sight line down her arm, past her rigid pointed finger, John saw a greyhound dog on the side of a large silver bus as it slowed down, making a right-hand turn onto the street behind the parking lot where he and Penelope were waiting.

"I love you, Penelope."

"I love you too, Dad." Whispering and keeping her eyes glued to the bus, Penelope said, "Here we go." She inhaled deeply and thought about the previous two days.

Penelope's initial conversation with her father had left her confused, angry, and with many questions.

"I have a sister? Like a real sister? How? Who? Where is she? Did Mom know? Dad?"

"I'm so sorry, honey. I know I should have told you before, but I didn't know how—and I wasn't sure if I would ever see her again. Before I knew it, well, time got away from me. I don't expect you to understand, but she will be here in a couple of days. She'll be with us for almost two weeks. We'll see how it goes."

We'll see how it goes? Penelope couldn't focus on anything her dad was saying beyond the fact that she had a sister. He was still talking, and it all sounded jumbled and a bit like the adults talking to Charlie Brown—wha, wha, wha. How old was she? Did Dad just say she was older? Two years older? Would they look alike? Would she like red licorice and Butterfinger candy bars? And why would Dad have kept her a secret?

"And you will have to share your room with her. We don't have the space, and the couch just won't work," Penelope's father continued.

"What? But what if she doesn't like me? I just don't understand why—"

"I know you'll be fine," John interrupted. "I trust that you will make it work. I'm counting on you to make this work, honey."

John's beseeching eyes quieted Penelope's verbal strike, and she went back to the questions forming in her head. What if she were one of those mean girls at school who would sometimes tease her about wearing the wrong clothes? What if her new sister didn't want a younger sister? They were only two years apart, but that could be an eternity when you were nine years old and your sister was eleven. But, having an older sister might be fun.

"Dad? Do you think she will even like me?"

"Absolutely. She will love you. I have no doubts about that, but I worry just like you. What if she can't forgive me for not searching for her all these years? Last I saw of her, well, she was little, just a toddler. When her mom left, I assumed I would visit. But they moved out of state, and I lost track. It's not an excuse, but I hope she can understand."

Shaking her blond head, Penelope just couldn't comprehend all the adult talk coming from her father. Again, she chose to speak to herself in her head, and her father seemed to be doing the same. They both had worries, fears, and questions that would be answered soon enough. Hopefully, the answers would find all involved happy about their future together.

Two days passed quickly. There was much to do: cleaning, worrying, questioning, more cleaning, grocery shopping, worrying, questioning, hoping, wishing, dreaming, and then more cleaning. Penelope's room had never looked so uninhabited. Everything was in its assigned place, and she had even found her other pink flip-flop, her favorite sparkling blue pen, three hair binders, and a bag of goodies received at a birthday party she had recently attended.

Crunching on the multicolored swirled lollipop found in the goodie bag, Penelope belly flopped onto her bed. She let her legs bend slightly and crossed her ankles as her arms splayed across the double bed, almost touching each side. This was her space, her palace and throne. The sanctuary where she read, wrote, did homework, and giggled on the phone with her best friend, Jennifer. It would now become a room for two, but not the having-my-friend-stay kind of sleepover. It would become a shared space—a possibly permanent shared, never-to-be-just-for-one space. Penelope emptied two dresser drawers for her sister as well as made room for her hanging clothes in the closet. This was not normal girlfriends hanging out. This was new and uncharted territory.

"I wonder if she will want space on my walls for her posters," Penelope asked aloud to no one in particular. "I could move my kitten calendar and take down my biography poster of Albert Einstein from last year." *The walls would become ours*, thought Penelope as she quickly tried to remove the *my* from her wonderings. Flopping onto her back with a clean sucker stick in hand, Penelope grinned, "I'm not sure I'm ready for this. But, ready or not, I have a sister!

* * *

Penelope couldn't keep her eyes off the Greyhound bus pulling into the station. She looked at each darkened window, wondering if CeCe could see her. It seemed unfair that she should see first, but there wasn't enough time to move further into that line of thinking because the bus stopped. With a whooshing sound, the door folded open.

An older gentleman wearing a white shirt and gray pants stepped off the bus first, followed by a woman holding an infant. It took forever for the next passenger to appear—an elderly woman with a cane cautiously walked down five steps. She looked up as the first older gentleman helped her down the final steep drop to the concrete. "Grandma!" shouted two young boys in unison, rushing forward to help their beloved visitor.

A skinny pair of legs appeared at the top of the stairs. The legs were attached to blue-and-white sneakers that paused before descending. Penelope and her dad reached for each other's hands at the same moment.

John's oldest daughter, Penelope's sister, finally reached the ground. She scanned the crowd, stopping abruptly as her eyes met the eyes of a father she had never really known. He was blond and wearing worn jeans and a white button-down shirt with sleeves rolled to just below the elbow. Slowly, she pulled her eyes from his to connect with the girl attached to his arm. An unwavering smile as big as CeCe had ever seen was spread across Penelope's face, making her eyes small slits. CeCe let a small grin squeeze out of her fear and stepped forward while her new family moved toward her. Their moment of waiting had ended, and they entered into a cautious new feeling of possibilities.

Penelope watched as her dad bent to rest on one knee, wrapped his long arms around his oldest daughter, bowed his head ever so slightly, and closed his eyes in prayer. CeCe's small arms prevented her from returning a full embrace, and she chose to give her father a small, quick squeeze instead.

Through tears, CeCe's father spoke first. "Hi, CeCe. I'm so happy to see you again. You are so beautiful." He stopped; he had lost his ability to speak.

"Hi, John," mumbled CeCe.

"My name is Penelope. I'm your sister," laughed CeCe's younger sibling. Penelope used the back of her hand to wipe the moisture from her own green eyes. "I've never had a sister before, and I always wanted one."

Both CeCe and John watched an enthusiastic Penelope and couldn't help but start laughing. Penelope's energy was contagious, and for a moment, the awkwardness faded; the girls hugged. Though previously unknown to each other, the sisters felt an immediate resemblance of face and spirit.

John grinned. "Let's go home. You must be hungry. Plus, we have so much to talk about. I'll get your suitcase."

"We are going to share my bedroom. Actually, it can be your bedroom now too. Do you like red licorice? I love it. And I really like chocolate, especially Butterfingers. What is your favorite kind of candy?" Penelope took hold of her sister's hand, continued questioning without waiting for answers, and led the family of three to begin a new adventure . . . together.

Chapter Two

The ride home flew by and along with it the worries of too much quiet and uneasiness. Penelope continued her quest with all sorts of questions while smiling nonstop.

The backseat of John's car had given CeCe the opportunity to examine the back of John's head. Occasionally, their eyes would meet when he looked in the rearview mirror. He smiled small, but his eyes begged her forgiveness while memorizing her face— just in case.

Penelope, on the other hand, seemed to have no hesitations. At times, she took CeCe's hand to further explain her thinking. The girls found that they had similar features: heart-shaped mouths, widow's peaks, and their father's cheekbones. They also could not ignore the obvious differences: Penelope was a blonde; CeCe was a brunette. Penelope had green eyes; CeCe had brown. Despite their difference in age, they were both about the same height. Even in the occasional silences, CeCe and Penelope had managed to find reassurance in each other. Their shoulders touched, and neither pulled away from the other.

Entering her new home for the first time was something she had dreamed of many times in her short life. For years, CeCe had wondered if she and John might meet, but then she had given up hope. Yet here she was. Everything was new, and it was hard not to stare at John, Penelope, and her temporary living arrangements.

"Who is this?" CeCe asked, referring to a picture of a toddler being kissed by a pretty young woman. The toddler's mouth was wide with laughter, revealing four little teeth. The picture held a place of honor above the television and was one of only a few decorative items around the sparse living room.

"My mom and me. I was two years old, and my mom loved kissing my cheeks. That's what Dad always says. I don't really remember, but that is my favorite picture."

"What happened to her?"

"When I was two and a half, my mom was in a car accident. She died."

"I'm sorry. I mean . . . I didn't know. I shouldn't have asked."

Penelope held the picture with both hands and smiled. "Don't be sorry. She's my angel now. It was a long time ago, and you didn't know." Penelope and CeCe stood side by side, staring at the perfectly captured moment.

The quiet was snapped when John yelled from the kitchen. "Girls, I have lunch ready. CeCe, I hope you like corn dogs with mac 'n cheese. Penelope chose the menu. It's one of her favorites."

Penelope walked with CeCe into the small kitchen containing a dinette set. There were four mismatched chairs, and the table was set for three. Looking around the kitchen, CeCe noticed that the beige refrigerator, green stove, and silver-speckled countertop were clean but had been well used.

John sat at one end of the red-topped chrome table while Penelope chose a chair across him. CeCe had no choice but to sit on one of the remaining seats between John and Penelope. She wavered. John either didn't notice her pause or chose to ignore her indecision.

"I love corn dogs. Watch. I swirl my ketchup and mustard around before I dip. What do you like to eat?"

Taking a nibble of her mac 'n cheese, CeCe responded, "I love corn dogs too. I also love cheese pizza, cheeseburgers, and Tater Tot hot dish."

"Me too! I like mushrooms and black olives on my pizza."

The girls smiled. John smiled. The conversation wandered around safe topics such as favorite color (blue for both), favorite animals (cats, dogs, and cows—cows for CeCe), and favorite TV shows (anything with singing or dancing).

"I have a gift for each of you," said CeCe when lunch was finished.

"We do too," Penelope and her father said in unison.

When CeCe returned from digging through her suitcase, she presented John with a deck of cards that said Nebraska on the back. "My mom said that you liked playing cards. I found these at the grocery store."

"Thank you so much, CeCe. I love them." John turned the deck over in his hands as if it were fragile and might break.

Turning to Penelope, CeCe placed a purple crystal-like rock in her hands.

"Oh my gosh. It is so beautiful. I love it."

"It is an amethyst from my rock collection, and it is my birthstone. I was told that purple is the color of wisdom. I hope you like it. It's not much, but . . ." CeCe didn't complete her thought.

"It is perfect and so sparkly pretty!" Penelope hugged her sister, and CeCe's arms responded in the same way.

"Okay. Let me get our gift for you," Penelope squealed as she released CeCe from their hug.

Penelope returned from the living room, clutching a wrapped gift. The paper was decorated with multicolored stars and hearts. Carefully peeling back the tape, CeCe opened the package. Her eyes gazed upon the first and only picture she had of her father and her sister. She stared at the faces in the frame that were smiling back at her. She had always wondered what he looked like. Now she knew and would always know. And now she was sitting in his kitchen. She looked up and whispered, "It is perfect. Thank you, both of you."

A hushed breath held the emotion of the moment, and for what seemed an eternity, no one said a thing. They each had their treasures and considered their value.

The phone rang and broke the silence. John jumped from his thoughts to answer the welcomed interruption.

"I'm sorry, Mae. We just got home, and I made lunch. She is fine. I'll put her on the phone." Each sentence was separated by Mae's questions.

John handed the phone to CeCe and motioned for Penelope to leave with him and give CeCe privacy.

*   *   *

Finally alone with just her sister and after a long day, Penelope asked, "Is everything all right with your mom?"

"Yeah, she just wanted to make sure that I was here and if I was doing okay."

While lying on a woven baby-blue floral blanket on their double bed, the girls stared at the ceiling while reflecting on the day. It had been filled with awkward pauses, the unpacking of clothes, and watching a little television. Supper had been a light salad, tuna sandwiches, and orange popsicles for dessert, which were eaten side by side on the front steps.

Penelope fluffed her pillow and turned to her right, facing her sister. "That was the best day ever. I am so happy you are here. I was really excited to find out I had a sister. I'm glad you are mine."

Quiet for only a moment, CeCe responded, "I am really happy to have you as my sister too. I wish we had known each other before today. I wish we could have—" CeCe stopped; her throat felt tight.

"Let's never forget, okay?"

"I'll never forget." Turning to face Penelope, the older sister took her younger sister's hands in her own and said, "Hey, let's make a memory. It is something my mom and I do when we share special moments. Close your eyes and try to remember everything we did and said today. Think about the smells and tastes. Remember the sounds and looks on our faces when our popsicles were dripping down our arms. I can still see your smile when we first met. Try it."

Penelope and CeCe lay in bed with their eyes closed, far from sleep. The events of the day were being firmly planted in their hearts and minds. Both girls smiled, made memories, and fell asleep facing each other while holding hands.

Chapter Three

Waking up next to someone they had never known was a new experience for the sisters. CeCe waited for Penelope to move before getting out of bed. "Good morning, Penelope."

"Uhhh. Good morning, sis," Penelope replied as she sat up, yawned, and stretched her arms above her head. Both girls looked at each other. "What should we do today?"

"Whatever you want. I'm game for anything."

"Well, we could ride bikes, go swimming, or play with my friend Jennifer."

CeCe quickly responded, "I don't think I want to go swimming. But the other two sound great."

"Okay." Penelope watched as CeCe's eyebrows scrunched, and suddenly, she didn't seem at all happy. Penelope hoped she hadn't done or said anything wrong already. "Are you okay?"

"I'm great. Let's get breakfast." And before Penelope could question any further, CeCe was up and walking toward the bedroom door.

*   *   *

Following a lively breakfast discussion about the best kinds of cold cereal, both girls agreed to go on a bike ride in order to explore the little town of Ironwood, Minnesota. Population: 435. CeCe used the bike John had borrowed from a neighbor for the duration of her stay, and Penelope had her own. Both bikes were the same size, each having banana seats and white baskets.

"Why didn't John come?" asked CeCe. She was unable to give John the title of Dad or Father. Only two years old when they were last together, she didn't even remember him. Now from out of the blue he wanted to be her dad. Dad was what you called someone who took care of you when you were sick. Dad was the person who taught you how to ride a bike or take you fishing. Early that morning, CeCe looked into the bathroom mirror while getting ready to brush her teeth and practiced saying John's name out loud. "Dad," she had said. No. "Father. Hmmm." No again. John seemed to work the best.

"He thought we should have some alone time. Plus, he has some errands to run, and then he wants to mow the lawn. Do you wish he would have come?"

"No, no. I'm happy with just the two of us. Race you to the corner."

After many races to corners, parked cars, and even trees, Penelope slowed down to point out the important buildings and homes in town. "This is Al's Café. He can be grumpy, but he lets me read comic books for free while I drink Orange Crush and eat cheese popcorn. This is the grocery store. Hardware store. Gas station one. Gas station two. Motel. Church. Church. Church. The policeman's house. Jennifer's house. This is the bakery and, finally, Anderson's Gift Shop—with the best selection of candy in town."

The sisters settled on the gift store for candy. The glass case held colors and treats of unbelievable range. They had only $1.15 to spend, with CeCe contributing the $1.00. Neither doubted that the money and the sweets were to be shared. No one asked; no one offered. Both emptied their pockets and combined their joy.

They managed to stretch their money and bought items that were sold two-for-one: two lipstick-shaped candies, two packages of Sixlets, two candy bracelets, and one package of red licorice.

Placing the bag of candy in CeCe's basket, the girls rode to a heavily wooded area of town. The forest air was jungle green, with overgrown brush, hardwood trees of every type, and noises from unseen creatures. One bumpy, rutted path led into the woods as if it were a sea monster growling with hunger, waiting to enclose the bikers upon their entrance into its enormous mouth.

CeCe let Penelope lead the way as it was her territory. Soon, it would become theirs, but for now, CeCe was content to play follow the leader.

Penelope braked at the remains of an old house. Three walls of the concrete block foundation stood, though they looked ready to topple at any moment. Dirt and growth from the forest floor had covered much of the space. It was one of those places that was visible only to those who knew it existed. People would walk by and not even notice. Only she knew the treasures it held, and she was willing to share them with her sister. Here they would make their own magical world.

Several bricks had been arranged into a low seat, with others creating a small flat table space. Penelope started collecting more bricks to make the space for two. CeCe, already of single mind with her sister, helped by brushing off dirt, bugs, and moss from the captured bricks. They were ready for their feast.

Eating candies from her bracelet, one by one, Penelope said, "Let's make this our fort. It can be our secret place. Sometimes, some kids ride through, but no one ever stops. I can hide here, and no one finds me. I haven't even told Jennifer about this place. She just wouldn't like it."

"I like it," CeCe mumbled as she used her lipstick candy on her already crimson lips. "We can make rooms. Right now, we are sitting in our kitchen."

Both girls broke out in matching giggles, like a zipper being pulled together. They laughed, ate, and imagined all the endless possibilities that a fort in the woods could afford.

*   *   *

Lying in bed on their second night together, the girls talked and laughed as lifelong sisters do. They made memories of their day together and promised never to forget their fort, candy treats, and an evening spent doing cartwheels and backbends in the front yard until the mosquitoes made gymnastics impossible.

John sat downstairs, reading the newspaper, and paused frequently to listen to his girls enjoy their time. *His girls*!

"Girls, time for sleep," he said with a smile. It was late.

Upstairs, the sisters shushed and placed fingers over their mouths, keeping their laughter muffled until they felt the need to throw the covers over their heads and make plans for day number three.

Chapter Four

The next two days revealed more of the same: riding bikes, meals with John, laughing, building of imaginary worlds on a forested floor, memory making, and a strengthening of sisterhood that rivaled siblings who had lived a lifetime together.

Summer must have wrapped her blankets around the breeze. It was sticky and still. It was the perfect day to create ripples on the mirrored surface of Round Lake. There are hundreds of Round Lakes in Minnesota, but this one had the best public beach. It was sandy with lots of space for towels and had crystal water. It also offered a simply constructed raft that floated four inches above the lake's surface. There were no ladders, but kids and adults alike lifted themselves up to rest, to visit, to rock, and to tip the raft of Ironwood.

Penelope whined, "Let's go swimming today. I'm so hot, and I want you to see me dive off the raft." To add drama to her request, Penelope laid the back of her hand on her clammy forehead and pretended to swoon.

CeCe had been dreading this moment. She knew it would happen. It couldn't be avoided any longer.

Peeking out from under her lashes, she softly trusted her sister with her secret: "I don't know how to swim."

That explains the look earlier in the week, thought Penelope. Staring directly into CeCe's eyes, Penelope spoke with assurance, "It's okay. We don't have to go if you don't want. But I took lessons, and I can help teach you. We can ask Dad to help—he is a good swimmer."

"No, don't ask John. I wouldn't feel . . . oh, you know what I mean. I want to, but I am scared. Maybe we—just you and I—can try it?"

"We'll go for just a little bit, and if you don't like it, we will come home." Penelope grabbed CeCe's hand, and together they gathered all the necessary items for the beach. They loaded Penelope's bike basket with a floral backpack containing threadbare beach towels advertising unvisited islands, sunscreen, and a thermos of icy orange Kool-Aid.

Pulling on shorts and T-shirts over their swimsuits, the girls hopped on their bikes. Enjoying the downhill breeze that came with riding to the beach, they flew with arms outstretched, feet off the pedals, and managed to hit the brakes in time to arrive at the landing.

There were at least a dozen kids splattering and splashing, trying to keep the heat from extracting all their careless energy. The girls marked their territory by placing their towels side by side and carefully putting their supplies on them. Slathering lotion from head to toe, they drank a little of their refreshing Kool-Aid.

"Let's just wade in up to our knees," suggested Penelope.

"I can do that," said CeCe.

The water was amazingly clear and felt as if the girls had entered into the walk-in refrigerator at Al's Café. Inhaling sharply, they wrapped their arms around themselves in an attempt to control their shivering.

"How about we go to our waists?"

Without waiting for her sister, CeCe nodded and slowly placed each foot one in front of the other over sand and an occasional pebble until she was in water up to her waist. She looked longingly at the raft and wished she wasn't so afraid. In the past, whenever she was in water deeper than her shoulders, she would panic and force her legs to push back toward the shore.

Penelope bent her knees and submerged herself under the water up to her neck. Tipping her head backward, letting the cool water slide off her hair, she couldn't help but let out a satisfying moan. "Ahhhh. This feels so good." She closed her eyes and smiled like she did when she was eating chocolate.

CeCe let water surround her shoulders as she too dipped farther under the water without going deeper. She wasn't quite willing to put her head under, nor was she willing to go into deeper water, not just yet.

Showing techniques learned during her swimming lessons, Penelope moved back toward the safety of the shore so that CeCe would be able to touch and see the bottom. Being in the shallow water gave CeCe the courage to try all that Penelope taught. As long as she could feel the sand squish between her toes, she was fine. She conquered dog-paddling quickly. Floating on her back was much more difficult. Lying back, CeCe lifted one leg and slowly pulled her other leg off the lake bottom. She jerked, gasped, and bent her body at the waist as if she had an anchor attached. She flailed in terror and her dread prevented any further attempts at floating.

"Let's save that for another day," said Penelope. "I'm proud of you. You can dog-paddle! Now try going a little bit deeper. Only go a little bit. I will stay right beside you. I promise."

CeCe hesitated. She trusted only a few people in her life, and here she was in water with a girl she had only known for a few days. Yet she knew that she trusted her with her whole heart. She would try for her sister. "Okay, stay close."

With bent arms and legs, CeCe cautiously worked her limbs together in a puppy version of a dog paddle. Her mouth was tight as she focused on the mission at hand. Penelope cheered, urging CeCe to continue.

"Keep going, CeCe. See if you can make it to the raft."

It was only six feet and she would be at the raft. It seemed miles away, but CeCe started her journey.

"You can do it," said Penelope.

Four more.

"Almost there."

On her last lunge, CeCe felt the fingertips of her right hand graze the side of the raft. As she raised her left hand above her head, it came down hard onto the surface of the raft with a spray of water. Gripping the edge, breathing hard, but with a smile in her eyes, she turned to face Penelope. "I did it!"

"I knew it. I knew you could."

Penelope swam to the raft next to CeCe. Both girls raised their bodies out of the water just enough to place their crossed arms on the top of the raft. They rested their heads on their arms while their legs enjoyed the coolness of the darker water below. Occasionally, their legs would rise back toward the sun just to create waves and compete for the biggest splashes from their wild kicks. Three other swimmers were on the raft, jumping in and out of the water as if on springs.

"Let's sit for a while before we go back," said Penelope.

The girls lifted themselves completely out of the water and sat on the edge. Swinging their legs, the sisters enjoyed the quiet calm of the moment.

"Do you think he is upset that we are here without him?" asked CeCe.

"Nah, he's fine. He's pretty quiet and likes to be at home. I'm sure he found plenty to do. Why? Do you wish he were here?"

"I'm fine," she said too quickly. Penelope did not pursue the issue.

"Hey! Do you guys want to tip the raft?" one of the springy boys asked the sisters.

Penelope knew "tip the raft" meant that everyone would stand on one corner of the raft until the opposite corner was high in the air. The results usually ended with mostly everyone losing their balance and falling into the water. However, knowing CeCe's swimming skills, Penelope thought it best to wait for another day to accomplish that feat.

"Thanks, but we are going back to shore. Wait until we get off, okay?"

CeCe's shoulders shrugged, and her head tipped to the side.

"As soon as we get closer to shore, watch what happens. Let's go back. Are you ready?" asked Penelope.

Taking a big breath, CeCe nodded and again trusted her sister. Both girls slid back into the water. CeCe hung on for as long as she could and pushed off toward the shoreline. The momentum from her push helped her speed toward more shallow waters. Her puppy paddling felt stronger and more confident.

Standing on secure sand again, CeCe released the breath she had been holding. Penelope placed her arm around CeCe's shoulders and spun her around to watch the activity on the raft. Several older kids had joined the others until there were about ten participating in the tipping. Everyone raced to one corner of the raft. Some kids hung on to others while some were bent at the waist with one hand on the raft, using it to balance. The submerged corner kept sinking while the raised corner soared higher and higher. Suddenly, the raft shot out from beneath many feet. Most kids went flying backward, landing like a giant group cannonball. Two lucky boys managed to maintain their balance and stay on the raft. They jumped up, pumping their arms in a victorious display of dexterity. The defeated swam back to the raft to try their skills again and again.

Wide-eyed, CeCe spoke first. "Whoa. I am so glad that you got me off of there." There was a slight shiver in her voice.

"It's so much fun but kinda scary too. One of these days, we'll do it together, but only when you are ready."

The sisters continued to play in the shallows, alternating between trying unsuccessfully to catch little minnows and swimming with two hands on the bottom, pretending to be snorkelers or sea monsters. Occasionally, they would return to their towels to rest, drink, and apply more sunscreen.

Other beach visitors came and went throughout the afternoon. It was soon time for the girls to head back home. Pushing their bikes up the hill was easier than trying to pedal with their water-tired legs. Damp, sandy towels were draped around their necks, and their flip-flops squeaked with each step.

"Thanks for going to the beach. I had the best day ever," Penelope said, pausing in her walk up the steep incline. Riding down had always been much quicker.

"I can't wait to go again. And you are right. It has been the best day—ever."

Finally reaching the top, the girls hopped back onto their bikes and leisurely rode home in a comfortable silence.

* * *

It was still steamy, oppressive, and motionless outside when the girls got ready for bed. A fan tossed the sweltering air around the room, and both girls chose to lie on top of the covers rather than face the furnace underneath. A slight rumbling could be heard in the distance.

"Is John on vacation while I'm here?"

"No, he decided not to take any jobs during your visit. He does lawn work and carpentry, and he even fixes people's cars. He has a lot of jobs, and he's really good at them," said Penelope.

"That's nice," sighed CeCe.

"Do you miss your mom?" asked Penelope, lifting her damp hair from the back of her neck and placing it higher on the pillow.

"Do you miss your mom?" CeCe questioned back.

Knowing the answers, neither girl replied nor felt slighted by the lack of response from the other.

"You know, if you want, you can always talk to Dad. I think you would like him more if you talked to him more."

"I'm fine," CeCe gruffly responded. Then quickly changing the manner in which she spoke, she added, "I have you—the best sister in the whole world." Pulling her pillow out from under her long dark hair, CeCe swung and connected with Penelope's midsection.

Caught off guard, Penelope was startled but reacted and mirrored her sister's actions.

Instantaneously, both girls were kneeling on the soft mattress. Pillows were swung, and targets were hit repeatedly. Each completed attack triggered squeals of delight. Loud in their battle, they didn't hear, nor did they see, what was beginning to brew outside their second-story windows.

BANG! It was like a dragster had fired its engines in the small bedroom.

Penelope stopped her advance to see if the bed was broken. Neither girl moved except to look at the other. When the light outside their bubble was as bright as daylight, realization took hold, and both girls screamed.

BANG! The thunder was deafening.

"Daaaaad! Daaaaad?" screamed Penelope. "I hate storms!" Dragging CeCe, Penelope ran to the edge of the stairs. "Let's go down and get Dad, okay?" Not waiting for an answer, Penelope grabbed the handrail and descended the stairs two at a time.

"Sure, but it's going to be all right, Penelope," CeCe said to Penelope's back as she tried to remain calm, both for herself and for her sister. She didn't mind a thunderstorm, but the quickness with which this one had started had her worried. *It wouldn't hurt to find John*, she thought.

Running wildly from room to room didn't take long as there were only four downstairs: kitchen, living room, bathroom, and John's bedroom. The girls couldn't locate the adult of the house. Penelope continued to call for her father as she went to the front door. As the girls stood side by side, another flash revealed John standing on the front steps under the awning, watching the sky. The flash that followed the previous was too quickly followed by another rumble of thunder. The storm wasn't close; it had arrived. The trumpet blasts from the heavens produced jumps and shrieks from both girls. John looked toward the door.

Calmly, John entered the house, let the screen door slam, and said, "Girls, get to the basement. Now."

The sisters nodded but didn't move. They were waiting for John to lead them to safety. "Okay, come on, we'll be fine. Penelope, grab the flashlight out of the junk drawer. I just put batteries in it the other day. CeCe, I want you to take the radio off the kitchen counter."

All movement in the house stopped as a loud wail seemed to reach louder decibels than either thunder or the racing of their hearts. They all knew that sound. It could mean only one thing—tornado.

"Now!" yelled John. Each girl moved into action and ran toward the basement door.

It didn't matter that only a lone bulb hanging in the middle of the unfinished ceiling lit the basement. It didn't matter that spiders the size of softballs lived in secret places. It didn't matter that the basement had a corner that was always damp from what Penelope could only imagine. Their safety mattered.

John tested and retested the flashlight that Penelope had carried. It worked. He tested the radio that CeCe had taken from the kitchen. It too worked. Pulling a frayed striped blanket from a small wooden cupboard, John laid the blanket on the floor next to a closet door. He motioned for the girls to sit as he adjusted the radio to a local station. Penelope sat without thinking of spiders. CeCe sat and quietly wished that her mom were with her.

The radio announcer urged all listeners in the vicinity of Ironwood and the surrounding area to take shelter immediately. He warned of a possible tornado sighting just west of town. A wall cloud was moving northeast at fifteen miles per hour. Penelope and CeCe only understood pieces of what was being said, but they knew they were scared. Holding hands, they watched John. He was the barometer upon which they measured their fear.

"I'll be back. Stay here," said John.

As he headed toward the stairs, Penelope pleaded, "Please, Dad. Stay with us. Pleeease. Don't go."

"I'm only going to check on—" Interrupted by another crash of thunder, John didn't complete his thought.

"Da—uh, John. Please don't go," CeCe asked in choppy breaths.

Penelope didn't catch the near mistake, but John did. Pausing with his hands on the railing, he turned toward CeCe. "All right, girls. I won't go outside, but I'm going to the kitchen to get a couple of things. I won't be gone but a minute, and you'll be able to hear me. One minute. I promise."

This was another promise that CeCe had been asked to believe, but from John, it wouldn't be as easy. It was not like trusting her sister while swimming. John hadn't kept any promises that a father makes to his daughter. He had left her, had given up on her, and he definitely didn't deserve to be trusted. She had no choice though. She nodded, and John bounded up the stairs, singing the entire way.

"Your cheatin' heart," sang John.

The song was unfamiliar to both girls, but his off-key attempts to keep them listening and knowing his location kept them calm. Penelope looked at CeCe and whispered, "He's a terrible singer, and he doesn't even care." She dared to let a strained laugh leak from her throat. CeCe did the same. However, never once did the sisters let their one hand become two.

John returned carrying apple juice, three cups, a box of crackers, and the cards given to him by his oldest daughter. CeCe noticed they were wrapped in a rubber band. *He's used them*, she thought.

For the next thirty minutes, John listened to the radio while the three played rummy and crazy eights. If the storm hadn't been whirling outside, the moment could have been completely enjoyable.

The sirens stopped about ten minutes after they had started, but the little family stayed safe until they were sure that life upstairs was secure. Reluctantly, they climbed the stairs and went to their respective bedrooms.

"Good night, Dad. I love you."

"Good night, John."

"Good night, girls. Try to keep the giggling to a minimum tonight."

Penelope had the last word. "We sure have a lot of memory making to do tonight, CeCe."

Chapter Five

After an exhausting and eventful night, sleeping late felt luxurious. By the time the girls had fallen asleep, it had been well after 2:00 a.m.

"Let's go, young ladies," Dad yelled cheerfully from the bottom of the stairs. "I want to take a ride and check out the storm damage. It was pretty bad just south of town. Maybe we can help."

Bright sunshine gave the day a new face. It was hard to imagine that the previous night had been witness to terrible storms blowing through the area. Through still-heavy eyelids, Penelope peeked at her sister, who was smiling with eyes closed. "Good morning."

"Good morning," whispered CeCe.

"Do you want to go with Dad this morning and look at storm damage? Maybe we can talk him into taking us to Al's for lunch."

"Sure. I wonder if the damage was really bad. It might be interesting, and going out to eat sounds great."

After dressing quickly and eating a breakfast of cinnamon and sugar toast, the three climbed into John's blue Ford Galaxie 500 and headed south of town. It seemed as if all that remained of the storm were a few branches, some leaves, and tipped garbage cans.

"Here we go, girls. Look on your left. Whew! Look at all the trees." Dad paused, awed by the devastation near Rice Lake.

"Oh my gosh," said Penelope.

Leaning forward, CeCe and Penelope stared wide-eyed out the left back window. Their mouths moved like that of marionettes, wooden with no emotion. The bare trees were hunched, as if bowing toward unseen royalty.

"That could have been straight-line winds. Do you see how the trees are all facing the same way? Tornadoes twist and grind like a blender," said Dad.

"Dad, look at that house. There's no roof."

"Is that a garage tipped over?" CeCe added.

As quickly as they had entered the storm's debris field, they left. The landscape resumed as if nothing had happened.

"Let's grab a bite to eat. Maybe I can talk to some of the guys at Al's to make sure no one needs our help. What do you think?"

Penelope looked positively pleased as her eyebrows jumped up and a grin spread across her face. Her eyes slid sideways as she responded, "Great idea, Dad. I wish I had thought of it."

Unsure as to why both girls were laughing, John returned to Ironwood and parked in front of a small café on Main Street. Large neon-red letters spelled out Al's Café. The lights in the *f* had burned out years earlier but in daylight were easily identifiable as Al's Café. The building had a redbrick bottom and windows on the front and side facing south. A double set of doors marked the entrance into one of Penelope's favorite places in town.

John held the doors as the girls entered the café. CeCe was unimpressed by the six simple booths that each could only seat four and the two large round tables with seating for six each. The impact of a small candy display was minor as was a small magazine-for-purchase area. But her sister's energy was infectious, so she held off on her judgment.

Penelope chose a booth next to the magazines while John joined a round-table discussion with three other men from town as well as the owner, Al.

"Girls, what would you like?" asked John from across the room. "Should we get the same thing, or do you want to order different things and share?"

Browsing through the two-page menu, CeCe told Penelope to duplicate her order. A gray-haired gentleman wearing a blue short-sleeved shirt with red suspenders and carrying a pen and pad of green paper approached the table.

"Hello, sunshine! It's been a while. I've missed seeing your smiley face. Where have you been, and who is this beautiful young lady sitting with you?"

CeCe listened and nodded as Penelope talked about her activities since last they had seen each other. Al sparkled as she spoke. He loved his customers, he loved his restaurant, and he loved creating an atmosphere of family in his little space in the world.

Adding to the conversation, Penelope continued, "This is my sister, CeCe, Al. Isn't she wonderful? I didn't even know, and she didn't know either. We just met, and she is just my favorite person already. Oh, and we'll have two Orange Crush pops, two cheeseburgers, and two pieces of strawberry pie with tons of whipping cream, please."

"I'll be right back, ladies. Nice to meet you, CeCe. You are one lucky girl. Your sister is a sweetie, and your dad is one of the nicest guys I've ever met."

"Thanks" was all CeCe could manage. She enjoyed meeting Al, but the comment about John had made her tummy tumble. Other people thought John was a great guy, so why was she having such a problem? She knew the answer to that question, and she knew why she had issues with John. She just wasn't sure that things would ever change.

Snapping out of her internal conversation, she looked at the comic books that Penelope had gently tossed onto the laminate tabletop. "I don't know what you like, so I brought a variety. Al lets me read them for free. I love *Archie Comics* the best. Pick one."

CeCe hadn't even noticed that Penelope had left the table. But somehow, comic books of every genre were in front of her, and *Betty and Veronica* momentarily diverted her attention. "I love this. I can't believe he lets you read them for free."

Sipping Orange Crush from large red plastic glasses, the girls were surprised when cheeseburgers were placed in front of them. Time had escaped while they were reading and enjoying their visit into fantasy worlds. However, the smell of a perfectly greasy cheeseburger brought them back to reality, and the comics were closed.

"Mmmm," groaned CeCe. "I didn't know I was so hungry. This is great. Pass the ketchup, please."

Both girls set to work turning their cheeseburgers into edible works of art. Red ketchup, yellow mustard, green pickles and lettuce, and scarlet tomatoes were added to their creations. Very little talking was to be heard at their table, and CeCe began to understand why Al's was a little piece of heaven in this special town of Ironwood. This understanding was forever cemented in her head and heart when two enormous mountaintops of white whipping cream supported by three-inch-thick strawberry pie appeared out of nowhere.

"Now that's what I call dessert," Penelope said with a wicked grin. Her finger couldn't help but swipe the peak off the mountain and pop it in her mouth.

Both girls burst out laughing when CeCe did the same. Eating pie with a sister is the best thing ever, and the girls knew it.

Following dessert, a debate took place over whether Archie should choose Veronica or Betty. Both agreed that Betty was the right choice.

The girls closed their comic books when John approached the table.

"Ready? It would appear as if the storm damage was limited to what we saw earlier. They have plenty of volunteers, so there is nothing we can do to help."

John continued, "How about we continue the card game we started last night, and after I win, we could watch a movie and have popcorn? We have to get up early tomorrow anyway. The Fourth of July parade starts at eleven."

"Let's do it," said Penelope, and CeCe agreed.

*   *   *

Each person won a hand of gin rummy at least once. The TV movie was a Disney cartoon that each had seen countless times but was enjoyed with as much gusto as the first viewing. The popcorn was perfectly buttered, salted, and lightly sweetened with honey. John was the best at tossing kernels into the air and catching them in his mouth. And when it was that time of night—just before the mosquitoes go out for dinner—the three sat on the front steps, and this time, they ate blue popsicles.

"Hey, look, girls. It's the first stars of twilight. There are three of them."

Three people sat mesmerized by the twinkling of stars in the northern sky, directly above the tree line, playing close to the moon. In the universal distances, they were light-years apart; however, from where this little family watched, they looked close. Like numbered stars in a dot-to-dot coloring book, all they needed was to be connected.

Chapter Six

Penelope loved the Fourth of July parade, candy, and picnic. But, it was definitely the fireworks that made this one of Penelope's favorite days of the summer. In her opinion, the first day of summer break from school was the best, and the Fourth of July was second. Penelope woke up early, shook CeCe from her deep slumber, and like a conspirator, said, "It's going to be the best day ever. I love fireworks!"

"What time is it?" CeCe shook her head. "You're crazy!"

"Come on, let's get ready. Let's wear red, white, and blue."

CeCe rolled to face Penelope, pulled the covers tight, and wrapped Penelope in a giant cocoon of blanket and sheet. "How's that for crazy?" she cackled.

Bouncing off the bed, the sisters ran downstairs to check on the plans for the day. John sat at the table, drinking coffee and reading the newspaper. "Good morning, girls. Happy Fourth."

"What time are we leaving for the parade? Do we have a picnic ready to be packed? Dad, are we coming back before the fireworks, or should we pack bug spray and jeans?" The questions were unrelenting, one after the other, without a breath, while John and CeCe watched words shoot like fireworks out of Penelope's mouth.

"I love fireworks!" Penelope proclaimed.

"Well, let's get ready then," John exclaimed, jumping from his chair and encasing Penelope in a bear hug from which she could not escape. Turning toward CeCe, he smiled and winked. CeCe gave a small smile.

The car was packed: two blankets, bug spray, sunscreen, swimsuits (just in case), towels (just in case), cooler (complete with six Colby cheese and bologna sandwiches, a large bag of Cheetos, a bottle of Coke with three glasses, and a package of Oreos), three lawn chairs, and a camera.

Parking the car only two blocks from the parade route in downtown Crosslake, John and the girls unloaded the necessary items for the parade—the first event of the triathlon day ahead of them.

John and Penelope always sat with Grandma Hazel on the corner in front of the antique store that Anna, Penelope's mother, had always loved. Grandma Hazel was Penelope's maternal grandmother, and John ensured that their relationship was a strong one. Penelope had frequent visits, during which they spent time picking raspberries, learning to knit, and even taking a few piano lessons.

The girls laid a blanket on the curb for themselves while John unfolded two green-and-white-webbed lawn chairs, one for him and the other for Grandma Hazel, who was waving at them across the street.

"Happy Fourth of July, sweetheart," Grandma Hazel gushed as she took Penelope's face in her soft hands and planted a kiss on her forehead. She and John gave each other friendly hugs. Turning to CeCe, she said, "Hello, CeCe. I'm happy to meet you. I've heard so many wonderful things about you. I hope we get to spend some time together." CeCe was swept into the warm arms of Grandma Hazel and also received a kiss to her forehead.

CeCe's heart smiled as she accepted and returned the welcoming hug. "It's nice to meet you."

As soon as she returned to creating the perfect space to watch the parade with Penelope, CeCe stopped. How had Grandma Hazel heard so many things about her? She had only known John and Penelope for a week. Who had been talking about her? It had to be John. Penelope was with CeCe every waking moment. What had John been saying to Grandma Hazel that she hadn't heard?

"Okay, let's split all the candy we get." Penelope broke the silence.

"Sounds good to me. Do you usually get a lot?" CeCe responded, shaking her own conversation from her brain temporarily.

"Sometimes. That's why I brought a bag."

Sitting side by side, the sisters waited for the parade to begin while John and Grandma Hazel talked—but not within earshot of the girls. Occasionally, CeCe would turn to look at John and Penelope's grandmother as they visited. One glance backward had CeCe feeling exposed. She had met with John's eyes for a split second. Something in CeCe's expression caused John's eyes to glisten and shine. His smile was brief and sad. CeCe turned back in time to see the Legion Color Guard turn the corner, indicating the start of the parade. Her eyes blurred as she joined the crowd and stood to pay respect to the American flag.

*   *   *

The parade was all that a typical Fourth of July parade should be. There were fire trucks, politicians, clowns, local high school bands, a few floats, and an ending with horses. The girls thoroughly enjoyed accumulating candy by the handfuls. Some candy was thrown directly into their ready hands, but more frequently, they raced other children a few feet out into the street. They agreed that the best float was Janice's Restaurant. Designed to resemble a building from the Old West, it even had a lower and an upper floor. There was a mock gunfight and lots of music. The crowd was impressed and clapped appreciatively.

The girls folded the blanket clumsily and said their good-byes to Grandma Hazel.

"Penelope, I wish I could join you for the picnic, but I can't today. I gave your dad a little fun money for you girls. I know how much you love cotton candy," grinned Grandma Hazel.

They all received another squeeze and kiss while expressing excitement about a visit they were planning to her cabin later in the week.

The second event of the day was a picnic. Stomachs grumbled as the car was moved closer to the park and unloaded again. The blankets were placed under the shade of a huge maple tree. Another family shared the shade, but the dark green of the maple provided plenty of protection from the sun for everyone under its umbrella.

With sandwiches, cookies, Cheetos, and beverages unpacked, the family of three ate as if they were at a fabulous banquet. Dad brought out the camera and captured his daughters in bouts of laughter, especially following an unexpected burp by his youngest.

"Would you like me to take a picture of the three of you?" asked the woman who was sharing the coolness of the shared shade.

"Thanks. We would love it," John said. Standing, he handed the camera to the kind woman and gave directions on how to use it.

John plopped himself down between his girls. He put his arms around each and pulled them in close. With a forced smile, CeCe endured the hug without saying anything. She was stiff in her posture and, as soon as the picture was taken, asked if John would take more pictures of her and Penelope.

Rising to retrieve the camera, John thanked the photographer and snapped shots of the girls in various poses. They laughed, looked sour, feigned sadness, went cross-eyed, and even made kissy faces toward the camera.

"Let's go to the beach. It's wonderful there, and it even has a lifeguard and a dock surrounding the shallow water," suggested Penelope.

CeCe responded with an overly animated "Absolutely!" She was eager to end the picnic portion of the day.

John told the girls to head to the bathrooms to change into their suits; he would wait for them under their tree. He said he wanted to rest his eyes. Both girls knew what that meant—nap! They were on their own for a while.

*   *   *

The beach and water was buzzing with kids. Families lined the shoreline with blankets and towels, with another layer enjoying the grassy parts of the park, just like John. Add to that recipe a bevy of boats and flags placed everywhere, and the scene was Americana at its finest.

The safety of a U-shaped dock provided CeCe with the courage to be more daring in her swimming exploits. She challenged herself to a high jump off the corner end of the wooden structure as her audience of one clapped for the Olympic athlete. CeCe did the same as Penelope performed a similar jump while pretending to pedal a bicycle. They were superstars in their field, and no one could compete against their God-given talents.

Hours passed in the perfection of a puffy cloud, blue sky day. At times, the girls would rest to watch skiers enjoy a breezy spray of lake water. Other times, they talked about *sister* things while watching other swimmers. They giggled at the teenagers who would sneak kisses when they thought no one was looking. Swallowing too much water, a young girl started crying. The sisters became bookends for her walk back to shore. Their connection was strong and cemented by trust and love. No one watching would have guessed that theirs was a weeklong relationship.

As the young girls were walking back to the mighty maple, hunger revisited them. John was talking to the adults seated on the neighbor's blanket when he spied his daughters.

"I was just thinking I should come and see if you girls were ready for something to eat before we find a spot for the fireworks. I checked on you earlier, and you seemed to be busy looking at boys," he teased.

"Dad! Stop it! We're hungry," Penelope laughed. CeCe's cheeks turned pink, and her eyes rolled as she vigorously shook her head back and forth.

Snuggled in their towels, the girls finished their gourmet sandwiches and licked the remaining orange Cheeto goo off their fingers. Oreos became an opportunity to play with their food. They blocked out their front teeth with the dark part of the cookies and laughed at each other's smiles. Parade candy was sorted, with the undesirables given to John.

Lying on their backs with watermelon Dum Dum sucker sticks poking from their mouths, the girls watched the maple leaves reveal the evening sky from between dances. Their drying wisps of hair swayed to the unheard music of the breeze. John watched in silence at the magic he saw before him. His girls. His daughters. If only CeCe—he couldn't think about that just now. *Give her time*, he thought. She just needs time.

* * *

Dressed in jeans, covered in bug spray, with a treat of pink cotton candy in hand, the girls sat in a new location for the last event. They chose their spot carefully for the fireworks. The slight hill would allow the three to lie back to watch the colorful display overhead.

Latecomers were filling into any available space as the time drew nearer to the show. Penelope commented for the fifth time about their *best* space as John and CeCe agreed and smiled for an equal number of times. Her joy and excitement were not to be denied. Grabbing at either her father's or her sister's hands, Penelope explained why certain fireworks were her favorite. Gold and falling like branches of willow trees were her preference for the moment, but that could and probably would change.

The park lights were darkened, forcing bugs to find other sources of illumination. "This is it," whispered

Penelope. All three sat up and awaited the initial explosion.

The crowd silenced as they heard an a cappella songstress ice the moment with "The Star-Spangled Banner" from somewhere on a distant stage. Rising, right hands placed on hearts, the crowd listened to the magic of the moment.

When the last word was placed before her audience, a series of six startling shots brought the crowd back to their original intentions; clapping and cheering came first, then the oohs and aahs began. For thirty minutes, the heavens were given the gift of color.

"Ohhh. Did you see that one? I love it! The colors look so bright," said Penelope.

"I love that one too. Wait. Ahhh. That one was so cool." CeCe was caught in the magical spell.

CeCe's and Penelope's eyes reflected the awe and excitement that fireworks bring to people of all ages. As the crowd watched the starry patterns and circular snowballs fill the sky, one person wasn't interested in what was happening above. He wasn't watching fireworks. He was caught in a mixture of sadness and guilt at all the fireworks that had been missed, of *all* that had been missed. He was angered by his choices that had changed the two lives of the people he loved most dearly. He tried not to think of the "what if" parts of his life. Going back was not an option, and somehow he had to make the girls understand that in order for their family to move forward. John just didn't know how to speak what his heart was saying.

*   *   *

The ride home was quiet; everyone was tired. They felt it in their arms and legs, but mostly in their mood. It had been an eventful day, and everyone needed the comfort of a pillow.

CeCe also needed the comfort of her mother's voice. "John, can I call home?"

At the mention of home, both Penelope and John looked up from the pile of remnants they had carried in from the car.

"Sure. We'll give you some privacy."

Penelope took John's hand and followed him to the living room. Snuggling with her dad on the couch, Penelope looked up at her father with tears in her eyes.

"Dad? Does she have to go home so soon? We are her home now."

Carefully choosing his words, John spoke honestly, "Yes, honey. She has two homes, and whether she comes back will be up to her and her mom. Our good-byes will come quickly, but maybe her return to us will also be quick. Let's enjoy our time together now. Don't worry about her leaving."

Both wondering how to do just that, father and daughter cuddled on the couch, leaning on one another.

*   *   *

When CeCe finished her conversation with her mother, she stood in the doorway of the living room to find John and Penelope on the couch. Awkward and feeling as if she might be intruding on a special moment, CeCe quietly backed out of the room to sit alone at the kitchen table.

Chapter Seven

With only four days and a wake up remaining, the girls set about the task of making a list of Fun Things to Do. Neither would talk about the fact that the list needed to get done before CeCe left. They just knew there was a lifetime of fun to cram into days.

Fun Things to Do

Fishing

Play with Jennifer

Swimming again

School playground

Make cookies

Paint fingernails and toenails

Visit Grandma Hazel

Remodel the fort in the woods

Camp out in the yard

Go to Paul Bunyan Park

Swimming even one more time

Stay up all night

Make a scrapbook—two scrapbooks

The list was posted on a cork bulletin board in their bedroom, and it was decided that as each thing was completed, it would be crossed off. There was room for additional activities if needed.

Jennifer was the first activity agreed upon, and a phone call revealed that she was free and would meet the girls after breakfast.

"I know you will like her. She is a really good swimmer, and she is a really fast runner. Her backbends and cartwheels are the best. Mine look dorky, but she never tells me," said Penelope. "She's also really good at basketball and softball. She has a lot of friends."

"I can't wait to meet her. She must be pretty special if you like her so much."

* * *

The three girls rode their bikes to the Ironwood Elementary School playground, which would allow them to cross two items off their list.

CeCe couldn't help but smile when she met Jennifer. She was energetic and incredibly friendly.

"Hi, I'm Jennifer. Some people call me Jenny though, but not Penelope. I can't believe that Penelope has a sister. I have three." Placing her arm around CeCe's shoulders, Jenny gave CeCe a hug. "We are going to be good friends. My sisters are younger. I have always wanted an older sister closer to my age. My sisters are just too young."

Penelope watched as Jennifer and CeCe talked and laughed. She was so happy that the two liked each other so much already. It would have been really hard if they did not get along.

With shoulder-length brown hair flying, Jennifer looked more like CeCe's sister than Penelope. Their conversation flowed smoothly, as if they had been friends for years. Questions and answers volleyed back and forth like an evenly matched game of tennis.

The girls rode their bikes right down the middle of the small town streets, knowing that traffic wouldn't be a problem. With CeCe in the middle, occasionally Penelope had a hard time hearing some of the ongoing conversation.

"What did you say?" Penelope asked, leaning forward on her bike so she could see the other two girls.

"Jennifer was asking about my farm," CeCe said, turning toward Penelope.

"Oh."

After two more attempts at trying to stay involved in the discussion, Penelope stopped. *It will be easier once we get to the school*, she thought.

The playground was typical of an elementary school: dome-shaped climber, one slide attached to a smaller jungle gym, a larger tubular slide attached to a larger jungle gym, two sets of swings, a baseball field, and a paved sidewalk perfect for chalk and games of four square.

Penelope suggested the monkey bars, but Jennifer wanted to talk more—so the swings were selected.

"Do you have a boyfriend?" Jennifer asked of CeCe.

"No."

"Me neither," offered Penelope.

"You goof, I know that," snickered Jennifer. "I was asking CeCe. She's older than us, so I thought she might have one."

"That's okay, Penelope." CeCe gave an apologetic smile to her sister. "No, I don't have a boyfriend. My mom would ground me forever."

"What's your favorite class in school?" asked Jennifer.

"Recess first, then I like gym. I suppose art is all right, and I'm good at math, but I don't care for it much," CeCe explained.

"I like art a lot too, but reading is really—" Penelope smiled but was cut off by Jennifer.

"I love gym too, oh, and recess. We are so alike," Jennifer piped in, talking over Penelope's words.

"Let's go to the monkey bars. I love to flip off of them," Jennifer said as she jumped off the swing and ran to the other corner of the playground.

CeCe smiled at her sister, gave her own swing one more push, and jumped off mid swing, landing on both feet and running after Jennifer.

At the same time, Penelope looked at her sister and returned the smile, pushed, jumped, landed on her feet, but lost her balance and crumpled onto her bottom. Getting up, she brushed the dirt and grass off her shorts and limped toward the others. Penelope felt the metal taste of blood in her mouth. Using her ring finger, the only finger without dirt, Penelope found where she had bitten the inside of her cheek. It would be fine, but more than her cheek and bottom had been bruised and hurt.

No one had waited for her, nor did it seem that they cared.

Arriving at the monkey bars, Penelope found CeCe and Jennifer were already sitting at the top with their legs swinging high above the ground.

"Come on up," said CeCe.

"I'm coming. Give me a minute," Penelope mumbled back to her sister.

CeCe's brow creased as she heard the change in the tone of her sister's voice. She couldn't think of what was wrong. "Are you okay?"

"I'm fine," Penelope grunted as she used her arms to maneuver one leg through the bars. Pulling her head and torso through, she was able to bring her other leg up and over the bar. She was now sitting next to Jennifer, and CeCe was seated on the farthest rungs.

"Hey, let's wave and see if we can get people to honk." Jennifer motioned the arm pull that is universal to truck drivers.

CeCe tried to involve her sister. "Sure. You okay with that, Penelope?"

"Yeah, whatever."

Traffic at this location was usually heavier than at any other in Ironwood. Highways 11 and 7 intersected across from the fence surrounding the school. It was the perfect place to watch traffic; Penelope had done it with and without Jennifer many times. Today, however, seemed slower than normal, and only a few honks responded back to the vigorous arm tugs.

Dropping through the bars, Penelope let the back of her knees grasp the cool silver metal, released her handhold, and abandoned the heads-up world in order to hang upside down. Gripping the bottom of her shirt and swaying slightly, she spoke her first words in at least ten minutes: "I love this. It's a whole different world upside down."

CeCe and Jennifer nodded at each other and joined Penelope by releasing their grasp of safety to swing beside her. CeCe looked at her close-eyed sister and knew she was making a memory. Joining her again, CeCe did the same and smiled.

Jennifer placed her arms next to her knees, slid her body back, and released her grip and flipped perfectly onto the ground. "Come on. Try it, you two."

"I can't. I've tried before. You know that," pleaded Penelope.

"I know, but I'll spot you. Come on. Try!" Jennifer kept pushing.

"No, I can't," Penelope choked back tears, and her voice sounded raspy, especially to CeCe.

"Okay, come on, CeCe. You do it. I know you can do it," said Jennifer, unaware of the way in which her words stung her longtime friend.

CeCe was aware though and ached for her sister. She knew what it was like to be fearful and unsure and, until only recently, didn't know what it was like to care for someone so deeply that her hurt became your own. "I can't do it either. I'll just hang here with Penelope for a while."

"Really?" asked Jennifer, shocked by CeCe's decision. "Oh, well."

Penelope and CeCe used their arms for support as they brought their legs down toward the ground. Both released and dropped the short distance onto the dirt.

"I'll race you two to the merry-go-round," shouted Jennifer. Taking a racer's stance, Jennifer popped off the imaginary starting line as if she had been snapped from a rubber band.

"Hey, I'm kind of hungry. Let's go home and see if John has lunch ready," suggested CeCe, turning to Penelope.

"Yeah, I'm hungry too," Penelope agreed as a rush of relieved breath escaped.

Noticing that she was alone in her race, Jennifer sprinted back to the girls. After CeCe told her of their lunch plans, Jennifer said, "Well, I should probably go home too. My mom and I are going shopping this afternoon. Let's play again before you go back," said Jennifer.

"Sounds great," said CeCe.

The girls rode home side by side at a leisurely pace, making their bikes avoid imaginary orange cones marking an unseen obstacle course. Jennifer was first to arrive. Giving hugs, the girls said their good-byes, and the sisters went home.

Making a quick lunch for themselves, the girls sat on the couch to wait for John to return from having coffee at Al's.

"CeCe?"

"Yeah."

"I'm sorry."

"For what?" CeCe placed her peanut butter sandwich back on its plate and turned her body to fully face her sister. Her legs were twisted toward the back of the couch, and she hugged her knees. This was serious.

"I just felt left out, and I didn't know if you liked her more. And then I couldn't hear, and I fell."

"You fell?"

"Yeah, but you didn't see. I bit the inside of my cheek." Penelope slowed her speaking and moved her eyes upward in order to look directly at CeCe. "I guess I was really just jealous. I didn't want you to like her more than me."

"I don't," pleaded CeCe, shaking her head. "I knew you were upset, but I didn't know why. And then I heard you. Well, when you didn't want to flip off the bars, I could tell you were upset, so I just sort of followed your lead."

"You could have flipped off the bars, you know."

"I know. But isn't that what big sisters are for?"

Blinking her eyes and swallowing the lump in her throat, Penelope hugged her sister with a might that was composed of relief, appreciation, and love. "Thank you so much. I love you, CeCe. You are the best sister EVER."

"I love you too, and you are the best sister EVER." Smiling at each other, their grins grew, and both relaxed. "Hey, promise me that you will always tell me what is wrong, and I will tell you."

"I promise, CeCe."

*   *   *

The girls spent the next hour waiting for John by pulling out markers, crayons, and various sizes and colors of paper. The distraction made time pass quickly.

"Girls? Are you home?"

"We're in the kitchen, Dad," answered Penelope.

"So what are your plans for the rest of the day?"

"Well, we have a list, and now we need to set up camp in the backyard"—Penelope lowered her voice—"and maybe you can tell us a scary story tonight."

"What do you think about this plan, CeCe? Beautiful pictures, girls."

"I'm fine with camping. Thanks." CeCe continued to draw her lake scene.

"Thanks, Dad." Penelope looked at her bumblebee. "I love bees."

"I guess I had better get the tent out of the garage, find the sleeping bags, and prepare to tell you the most horrifying story. Maybe I'll sneak out to the tent in the middle of the night and scratch on the side. Oooo." John wiggled both hands in front of their faces.

"Funny, Dad, but I don't think the neighbors will be too happy if we are screaming in the middle of the night."

"Yeah, you are probably right. I will have to put the rubber snake back in the basement."

CeCe heard the teasing, but her stomach churned at the thought of being scared. She wasn't too sure about the story, but middle-of-the-night scratching on the side of a tent sounded downright frightening. Penelope didn't look scared, but maybe she liked scary things.

* * *

Setting up the tent in the backyard seemed best as the front yard was lit up each night by streetlights. Plus, the backyard was private, so the girls would be less likely to have uninvited neighborhood visitors.

The tent for two was perfect. The three worked together to pull cording tight and knot it firmly around the loops of the metal stakes. Penelope tied back the door flap in order to air out any musty smells hiding in the corners of the long-ago-used camping gear. CeCe hung the sleeping bags over clotheslines to freshen and grabbed a few extra blankets, just in case they need cushioning or it got cold. John went into the house to start on a great dinner for them to eat.

"Hmmm. What else do we need?" asked Penelope to no one in particular.

"How about flashlights?" CeCe offered.

"Yup, good idea. I know where there are two. I'll be right back." Returning only a moment later, Penelope was carrying two flashlights and the portable radio. Also, hanging from around her neck, Penelope had found a pair of binoculars.

"Look at this stuff I found." Penelope was beaming, as if she had true treasure to behold. It did seem like a fortune to both girls. Flashlight switches were switched, radio-tuning knobs were tuned, and binoculars were adjusted in order to see deep into the small grove of trees behind the house. The girls took turns with each gadget. They found the binoculars to be particularly entertaining, especially when looking at each other at close range.

"All right, your picnic dinner has arrived. I have packed enough food and pop to feed twenty campers," Dad moaned as he pulled and tugged at the red cooler loaded with goodies. Then as quickly as he feigned a struggle, he picked up the evening's supplies and delivered them to the camping princesses with a great bow.

"Thanks, Dad."

"Thanks, John."

It was still light outside, but the girls wanted to change into longer pants before they ate and settled in for the evening.

"Remember, no running in and out tonight. Get what you need, and then only for necessary reasons do you come back to the house." He grinned. "I'll come back with a story when it gets dark. Beeeeeeeee reeeeeeeeeady."

* * *

Properly dressed and prepared, the sisters laid the sleeping bags unzipped and open on the bottom of the tent. The extra blankets, smelling of summer sun, were laid on top to create a cushion that felt as plush as goose down. They decided it would be more fun to share their sleeping space rather than to be moths in their own cocoons. A small rug was placed at the entrance to their palace, and their evening meal was brought inside.

Crunching on hors d'oeuvres of carrot and celery sticks dipped in ranch dressing, the girls listened to music. The radio stations changed as often as the disc jockey spoke. There was much discussion about the joys of rock 'n roll, country, and pop music. The girls loved it all as long as they could sing. Even when the words were unknown, the sisters made up their own lyrics or laughed at their mistakes. They were never embarrassed. It was an acceptance and a knowing that the other was to be trusted with silliness, with serious thought, and with all that each chose to be. They were sisters.

Dinner's first course was followed by cheese quesadillas wrapped in tinfoil, which kept them warm. The cheese was perfect—not too thick but just gooey enough. Next, it was time for the dessert course. They enjoyed two large pieces of chocolate cake with thick, fluffy frosting, which John must have made earlier that day to surprise them.

"Mmmm. Chocolate cake is my favorite. I could have it every day." CeCe licked the frosting off the back of her fork.

"I wish we could eat it every day—together," said Penelope as she used the back of her fork to combine the remaining crumbs for a final bite.

Both knew what Penelope meant by *together*, but each chose to save that discussion for later. Tonight was meant for fun and not for the sadness that was to come in only a few days.

The thermos of pop was brought out to finish their feast. Plastic glasses, complete with Orange Crush, were brought together in a toast.

"To us!" the sisters chimed in unison and drank until orange-colored mustaches and bubbly burps appeared.

*   *   *

Night slowly positioned her moon and walked it across the night sky. The three stars of twilight reappeared, and John fulfilled his promise to return and tell a story.

"Once when I was young," John started his story as his wide-eyed daughters sat straight with blankets huddled at their mouths, preparing for a possible scare. He sat just outside the screened and zippered door, barely visible; his shadow was an outline against the night sky. Only when his eyes widened was his face discernible.

He continued. "I was with my brother, your Uncle Stanley, and we lived in a two-story house on a small farm in North Dakota. We were a long way from town, and the rest of our family was gone for the weekend. We were young, maybe about nine and eleven, like you girls. Can you imagine being home all alone for a weekend at your age?"

The girls moved their heads from side to side and didn't say a word.

"It was a different time. We *thought* we would be fine, but we didn't *know* about our house." Letting the words create pictures in their minds, John waited a moment.

With teeth clenched and eyebrows high, the sisters pulled the blankets even higher, with only their noses and eyes exposed. "What happened next?" dared Penelope. She had heard many of his stories, but this was a new one saved for a special occasion. It was going to be good and scary; she just knew it. Her own heart was racing, and CeCe's could be felt where their arms touched.

Slow and methodical, John continued, "Stanley and myself had just done chores. You know, milking and feeding the cows and cleaning the barn. We cleaned ourselves up, had a little bite to eat, and went upstairs to go to bed. Neither of us could sleep. It was hot, and our bedroom was stuffy and uncomfortable. I asked Stanley if he wanted to play cards, and he agreed because we weren't falling asleep.

"It was dark outside. Not like tonight. It was one of those nights when the moon is small and the stars are hard to find. There was so little light. In fact, it was pitch outside our one little window. I just shiver when I think about what happened next." John let out a choppy oooh as he shivered with great drama.

Unblinking, the girls let bite-sized squeaks escape. It was exactly what John had in mind. He bent closer to the door, took a deep breath, readying himself. His silhouette seemed to be growing right before the girls' eyes.

"I'm sure I was winning. Stanley was never good with cards."

"Daaaad! What happened?" Penelope's impatience won out over her fear.

"Can you see two young boys sitting on a large braided rug playing crazy eights? We had locked the front door downstairs and the door that was at the back of our bedroom that led to a rickety stairway at the back of the house. That door was to be used during emergencies only. We had also closed the door that led to the staircase leading to the living room. We were snug and safe, or so we thought." Another pause for dramatic effect guided the girls into deep nasal-sounding breathing into their blankets.

"Suddenly, we heard someone, or something, walk up three steps. The footsteps were slow, like *boom*, *boom*, *boom*. The sound stopped as suddenly as it had started. Stanley and I looked at each other and didn't move. We were listening hard. We had moved our heads so our ears could pick up any sound coming from across the room. I can still see the cards in our hands.

"'Ahhh. It's probably just the creaking of this old house,' Stanley told me, but it still felt wrong and weird.

"Nothing was happening, so we just returned to our card playing when we heard the footsteps again. This time, they came up three more stairs, but faster. *Boom. Boom. Boom.* And this time, we were really scared. Stanley let the cards drop from his hands onto the rug. They were facing upward. I remember because I would have won that hand." John smiled slightly, his silhouette turned toward the girls. "I wonder what you two would have done. Would you have screamed or sat in fear like we did?" Giving the question a moment to spin around in their child minds, he continued uninterrupted.

"Again the footsteps had stopped, but this time they didn't wait as long to move up toward us—four steps this time . . . *boom* . . . *boom* . . . *boom* . . . *boom*." The storyteller slapped his knee with each footstep.

"My brother decided to be courageous after the footsteps stopped again. He stood up, placed his hands on his hips, and yelled toward the footsteps. 'Come on up if you dare!' He said that. Can you believe it? What was he thinking? I wanted to run, but I couldn't move—and then he dares who-knows-what to come on up. I felt sick and sweaty." Letting this last piece of information sink even deeper into the girls' fear, John placed his face right against the mesh. With each breath he took, the flimsy door moved back and forth.

"The footsteps started again, but this time they were faster than at any other time. They didn't stop until the top. *Boom. Boom. Boom.* Whoever was on the staircase had now stopped right outside our bedroom door."

The sisters quit breathing and froze.

"The doorknob turned slowly. Slowly. The heavy old door creaked and groaned as it was opened inch by inch. Stanley and I waited for what seemed like an eternity. All at once, the door was pushed open hard, and AHHHHHH." John lurched forward to grab at the feet of his daughters.

Screaming and clutching at each other, CeCe and Penelope dropped their blankets. It was as if they were plummeting down the steepest roller coaster—arms were raised quickly, mouths were open wide enough to view tonsils, and bottoms rose off their seated positions.

John was laughing so hard his eyes moistened; however, he found time in his joy to calm his girls. "It's all right. It's okay. Sorry, I just couldn't help myself."

Heartbeats slowed, shrieks turned to rapid breaths, and unblinking eyes caught up to their needs. CeCe found the courage to look at Penelope, who looked back at her sister. As if given a cue by a director, they broke open their fear in a relieving rush of laughter.

"That was the best ever, Dad!" admired Penelope.

"I was so scared," said CeCe.

John stood, brushed imaginary lint from his shirt, and said, "My job is done. Good night, girls."

"Hey, wait! Dad, who was at the top of the stairs? Who opened the door?" Penelope asked.

"No one, sweetie. There was no one there. Your uncle and I screamed, unlocked the back door that led outside, and slept the rest of the night in the barn. Have a great night," he said, walking away toward the house.

"Was that a true story?" CeCe inhaled again deeply.

"No, he always likes to leave us thinking. We should ask Uncle Stanley when we see him. That was his best ever though. I got so scared."

"I don't think I'll be able to sleep."

"We will be okay. We can protect each other, plus we can always sneak inside if we want. Let's eat some red licorice," Penelope said while opening the door to reach inside the cooler.

Lying on their stomachs, calves and feet crossed in the air, the sisters used the red licorice as straws to drink the remaining Orange Crush. They pulled out notebooks and pencils and used their flashlights to spread a yellow beam across their writing. They wrote lists of favorites—favorite ice cream flavors, favorite books, favorite teachers, and so many more. Their knowledge of each other grew with each list, and they found so many similarities. The favorite best friends list was the preferred since both girls placed the other at the top.

After one last visit to the bathroom and final good nights were said to John, the girls returned to whisper in the dark. They created finger puppets that resembled real and imaginary animals that danced on the sides of the tent and told stories that featured each creature.

Conversation eventually gave way to droopy eyelids, and conversation slowed to a crawl.

"I love you, CeCe. It was the best day ever, again," Penelope managed to say.

"I love you more, Penelope." With those final words, CeCe fell asleep.

Seated just beyond the tent, John inhaled from the cigarette in his right hand and listened intently to ensure that his daughters were sleeping before he dared to venture indoors for the night. He didn't want them knowing he had listened to their fun or had checked on them. They were independent and strong young girls, but they were still girls—and they were his to protect and love.

Chapter Eight

"We crossed three things off our list yesterday," said Penelope as she put a red line through *camping*, *school playground*, and *Jennifer* on their master list. With a flourish, she placed the cap on the marker and turned to face CeCe.

They awakened early after a restful night's sleep. Following breakfast with John, who teased just a little about the previous night's screaming, the girls went upstairs to get ready for their day of fishing and a sleepover at Grandma Hazel's cabin on Sunfish Lake.

"I use to fish with my grandpa all the time," said CeCe while pulling and twisting her thick hair into a still slightly damp ponytail.

Penelope did the same. As fisherwomen, they both knew that hair in their faces would not mix well with bait and hooks.

"I even have my own tackle box at home," continued CeCe.

"I wish it was here. We could put all our lures together and have the best tackle box ever," giggled Penelope.

"Maybe I'll bring it next time," CeCe said without thinking.

Both girls stopped as the realization of those simple words had been said out loud into the universe for all to hear. Neither knew how to start a real conversation about the subject, so both remained quiet.

Penelope could only hope that her sister really meant what she had said.

Packing an overnight bag, CeCe began wondering about her comment. Did she want to return to Ironwood? Return to her sister? To John? Was her growing love for her sister enough to overcome her doubts about John?

* * *

Grandma Hazel's cabin was located on Sunfish Lake, ten miles out of Ironwood, and could only be visited by traveling a series of twisting dirt roads with green canopies. Several of the roads were meant for one vehicle. When two cars met, both would have to move far off the rutted dirt path. This interaction usually resulted in friendly waving by both parties. Signs with family surnames were nailed onto trees indicating directions to cabins that might otherwise be missed. A section of old barn wood with the name of *Johnson* painted in bright blue pointed left onto an even smaller side road. CeCe and Penelope had lost their way quite a few turns earlier, but this last left revealed the blue of a lake peeking through on the horizon. The road widened to reveal a large grassy area, and their cabin destination was perched on a hill overlooking the lake.

Grandma Hazel was using a broom to beat the dust and sand from rugs hanging on a single clothesline located at the back of the cabin. Giving a final smack on a blue braided runner, Grandma Hazel walked to the car to greet her guests.

Penelope, CeCe, and John smiled and gave hugs to the warm woman wearing a cotton floral dress protected by a soft yellow apron. Simple white tennis shoes with smudges of grass stains completed the outfit. Her short gray hair was striped with white in several places and was cut short for efficiency and ease. Numerous wisps were damp and curled onto her tanned forehead.

"You three picked a perfect day to visit. Look at that lake. It is so calm and beautiful. The fish are just waiting for you girls to catch them," she laughed and sparkled while patting her tummy.

"Get the gear, girls." John motioned to the car as CeCe and Penelope ran to gather poles, bait, and a bucket to fit the fish they hoped to catch.

"We'll be on the dock," Penelope yelled over her shoulder, already heading toward the lake. CeCe fell into line and followed the leader to the water's edge.

Looking down at the short wooden dock and calm of Sunfish Lake, CeCe fell in love with the setting. She had been to many lakes in her eleven years, and most of them were beautiful. This site felt different. It was quiet, simple, and felt like home. There were no boaters or fishermen at the moment. In fact, there were only a few cabins that could be seen from this view. The lake cornered, leaving parts unseen. Across the lake were pines of all types and even a small pasture with horses grazing. It was a scene that artists paint and about which poets write.

CeCe watched her sister take the slightly steep grassy hill instead of the concrete steps and descend toward the water. CeCe did the same.

The girls worked without speaking, and they efficiently prepared for the task ahead. The fisherwomen knew what to do. They partially filled the bucket with lake water for their catch to come. They examined their rods and made sure they were weighted while hooks were baited for the first launch of fishing line out into the quiet waters. Hooks and bait sank far enough below the surface, hoping to entice sunfish, perch, crappies, and even a few walleyes to check out the free lunch. Red and white bobbers nodded patiently, waiting to be dunked, which would indicate a possible bite on each girl's line.

Both CeCe and Penelope first chose worms as bait. Neither the squirming creatures between their fingers nor the leeches still to come bothered both girls. Standing on the dock, they each took turns casting in different directions. They were aware that if they chose the same course, their lines could tangle, creating a huge mess.

Water rings spread outward from bobbers atop the glassy surface. On the hilltop, John watched from the comfort of a lawn chair, deciding to let the girls enjoy themselves. He would join them soon. Grandma Hazel brought out lemonade and joined John.

On different occasions, each sister looked up toward her audience. Penelope waved; CeCe preferred to smile. The spectators returned waves and shouted words of encouragement.

Penelope was the first to get a bite. An unseen force pulled her bobber under, and she went into action. "I've got a bite, CeCe."

CeCe checked her own line and offered her help. "Are you all right? Yell if you need anything, okay?"

"Thanks, sis." Penelope played with the tautness of her line, first pulling, reeling, then releasing just a little at a time. She was teasing the underwater captive into an even firmer grasp on her hook.

"Aha! I have got it," she pronounced. Carefully reeling in her catch so as not to lose it, Penelope used her hand to pull up the golden-bellied sunfish from its watery depths. It wasn't the largest sunny she had ever caught, but it was definitely worth keeping.

"Nice work. She's a beauty," congratulated CeCe. "Hey, I think I have a bite too."

"Woohoo! Bring it in, CeCe," Penelope commanded. She wrapped her left hand around her fish, pushing fins downward to avoid puncturing her palm. Her right hand expertly pulled the barbed hook from the mouth of the fish, and she slid dinner into the prepared bucket. Penelope pulled another worm from the dirt-filled white Styrofoam container while CeCe reeled in a perch from out of the weeds on her side of the dock.

"Dad! Grandma! We already have two fish," Penelope shouted her own approval. "Come on down."

Agreeing that they should join in the fun, John carried rods and tackle for both himself and Grandma Hazel. She carried the two lawn chairs. Both chose the stairs.

After everyone was situated, serious fishing began. There was very little talking, usually only a quick congratulations or an offer of aid. Eventually, the girls took to sitting on the dock, letting their toes plunge in and out of the coolness. Hours passed as quickly as a snow day from school in the middle of winter.

"Grandma? We have, um, let me see, nine sunfish, three perch, and one nice-size northern. I say we take a break and have a little lunch. What do you think?"

John rubbed his stomach in a circular fashion and agreed. "Yup, my stomach is talking louder with each minute. Pretty soon the fish will quit biting altogether, because of the deafening rumble." He patted his tummy as if burping a baby, and everyone joined him in laughter.

Timing for lunch was perfect. It was that hour of the day when even the fish swim deep, next to the coolness of the mud bottom, to take a nap. After the bait was covered and the rods secured, John carried the evening's meal back up the steps toward the cabin. Grandma Hazel followed with the chairs while the girls ran up the grassy hill, slowing only as they neared the steeper portion at the top.

Entering the cabin for the first time, Penelope went straight for the refrigerator and grabbed a pitcher of water. Next, she took down two glasses from the cupboard next to the sink and filled them. The girls drank, wiping the moisture from their mouths with the backs of their hands.

Penelope gave CeCe a tour of the beloved family cabin. Entering from the outside, visitors were greeted with a small kitchen containing the basics. Dishes were done by hand in an olive-green plastic tub placed inside a white porcelain sink. The sink connected to a matching drainboard containing a single coffee cup, a small plate, and three pieces of silverware.

The kitchen was open to a dining room with a small rectangular oak table. Two chairs were placed on one side, with a red button-tufted, padded bench along the other.

The dining room exposed what could only be called a living room. The undersized space held just two larger items, a brown leather love seat wearing a multicolored afghan and a brown leather chest that sat low from the ground. Its purpose was obviously that of a footstool; however, it currently held three books.

On the wall above the love seat hung several pictures in various-sized frames. CeCe recognized John, Penelope, and Anna in many of the pictures.

Just off the living room was a small bedroom with a double bed and mirrored dresser. A handmade quilt graced the top of the bed in diamonds of purple and blue.

Another bedroom was located on the other side of the living room. It too had a homemade quilt with a central star of white and blue. Two mismatched dressers were on either side of a window framed with white lace curtains.

The only bathroom contained a toilet, sink, and a shower. An open shelving unit over the tank of the toilet stored necessary bathroom items.

Penelope's favorite room, and soon to be CeCe's too, was the massive front porch that ran the entire length of the cabin. It faced the lake and was wrapped in windows on three sides. The large glass windowpanes opened upward and latched to hooks on the angled ceiling. The screens let breezes cool the entire cabin. Two wrought iron daybeds spent their existence watching sunsets from across the lake. The most distinguishing feature of the room was the space between the bottom sill of the windows and the wood floor. The entire space was shelving filled with books of every shape and size. This room was the ideal haven in which to spend a cold evening, a rainy day, or even a sunny morning. Whether for sitting, sleeping, or reading, the room's many purposes made it the preferred and most loved of all.

"Grandma, can we eat in the porch?"

A distant unclear response came from the kitchen, but Penelope already knew the answer.

The girls pulled out two metal folding trays and set them up next to each other.

"I love this room. I love this cabin. In fact, I really love it here. You are lucky, Penelope," said CeCe.

"*We* are lucky. You are my sister, so this place is yours." Penelope smiled and threw her hands into the air, spinning around twice.

CeCe hadn't thought of it quite like that, but Penelope was right. She may not be Grandma Hazel's biological granddaughter, but as John's daughter and Penelope's sister, she could visit when they did, which she hoped would be often. However, that would mean visiting John often too. At this point, she wasn't so sure that was going to happen.

*   *   *

Lunch on the porch was filled with exaggerated fishing tales of previous years. Over potato salad, cold beans, and ham sandwiches, all four were eventually teased and felt comfortable teasing the others. Even CeCe found herself joking good-naturedly with John.

"There is no way you caught a two-pound sunfish last week, John. I saw Penelope roll her eyes. Her face says it all." CeCe shrugged her shoulders in an obviously humorous attempt at taunting.

"What?" said John, wearing a shocked look on his face. "You mean Penelope rolled her eyes at me?"

The sisters looked at each other and shook their heads vigorously back and forth. "No!" they said together.

"I was talking about your fish story, not Penelope's eyes," laughed CeCe.

As soon as lunch was done, Grandma Hazel went outside and quickly returned.

"All right, girls. If you catch them, you have to help clean them. Follow me," said Grandma Hazel, holding a clean bucket of water. She walked toward the back of a small shed.

"I love to catch them, and I love to eat them, but I hate cleaning them," Penelope whispered to CeCe.

Nodding, CeCe agreed, "I hate the mess."

Regardless of their true feelings, they would never have argued with Grandma Hazel's logic, and the girls obediently followed while John offered to clean up after lunch.

The side of the shed had seen many fish cleaned in its lifetime. A Formica tabletop on hinges dropped down, producing an outdoor workspace. Returning from inside the shed, Grandma Hazel had a stack of newspapers, a rather menacing-looking knife, and two fish scalers. She went back and retrieved a large garbage can and the bucket of fish caught earlier that morning.

"We will eat well tonight," said Grandma Hazel as she took a sunfish from the water and placed it on newspaper. She repeated the process two more times in order to set up each girl with a fish to scale. Grandma Hazel would do the dangerous job of using the knife to take off heads and empty each fish of its inside organs.

The sisters had both scaled fish before and knew that scraping off scales was a messy job. Both were careful to scrape away from each other. Scales fell onto the newspaper, went flying off the tabletop, and splattered against the side of the shed.

Grandma Hazel had also done her job many times before, and it took just a short time for them to finish. Garbage and fish parts were wrapped in the now sloppy newspaper and thrown. The freshly cleaned fish were rinsed in the clean water and placed in a glass Pyrex bowl to rest in the refrigerator until suppertime. John brought out a fresh bucket of soapy water. It arrived in time to scrub the tabletop and the side of the shed. Grandma Hazel hooked up a hose, and the final step was to spray the soapy water and scales onto the grass.

"Whew. I'm hot and stinky," said Penelope to herself.

"I would agree with that," teased John. He plugged his nose and used his left hand to wave away imaginary fumes.

"I can help with that problem," said Grandma Hazel. She turned the hose toward her granddaughter and let a small spray squeeze through the nozzle.

"Maybe I should hug you," Penelope laughed, stepping closer to her dad.

"Oh no, you don't," he said. "Let's go swimming."

The water at the end of the dock was only three feet deep, which took all pressures off CeCe to show her new swimming skills in front of John and Grandma Hazel. She thought the latter would understand and even help her, but she didn't want John to know she was unsure of herself in the water.

John and Grandma Hazel swam out past the dock to seek refreshment in deeper water. CeCe and Penelope jumped off the dock at least a million times. They never tired of finding an assortment of ways to generate the largest splash. Running from farther distances, curling their legs under themselves before they jumped, flailing about wildly in midair—all variations and more were attempted.

The adults retreated from the lake to sit under an old and large oak tree. The tree's branches were high enough that a small fire pit sat in its shade too.

The sisters continued to play and swim. Needing an occasional break, they would lay on their stomachs on the warm dock to watch life resume in the shallow water following its human disturbance. Looking between the slats of the dock revealed a world much different than the parts of the lake that received sunshine. Snails, bloodsuckers, and slime dwelled in the shade while sand, minnows, and small sunnies found comfort with sun.

It wasn't until called to get ready for dinner that the girls finally emerged from their adventure. Their noses and shoulders were pink from the heat but not burned.

Grandma had marinated the fish in lemon, olive oil, and a mound of green spices. John had helped by cleaning and cutting fresh potatoes and onions to be fried in one of the two black iron skillets.

The girls changed for dinner and hung their swimsuits on the clothesline. Taking a break, they stretched out on two long lounge chairs to relax and unwind before supper. The sun's angle in the sky forced them to squint while staring at the lake's shiny surface. The lake was still calm, but its color was lighter, as if trying to drain the last bit of blue daylight from the sky. It didn't take long before both were forced by fatigue to keep their heavy eyelids closed. They let the remaining sunlight warm them inside and out like a hug from a sister.

*   *   *

John and Grandma Hazel made dinner and let the girls sleep. It had been a busy day, and a nap was advisable if they were going to stay up late again, this time for a surprise campfire.

"Girls," John said softly. "Girls, I'm sorry, but we ate all the fish. You'll have to eat liver tonight." John pulled on their big toes as he spoke.

"What? Oh, Dad. You did not. How long were we asleep?" Penelope rubbed her eyes and stretched her arms, bringing about a wide yawn. "Arrree wu wake?" she asked CeCe, gently poking her upper arm.

"What did you say? Try it again, but this time without the yawn," giggled CeCe, peeking from between her eyelids and poking her sister right back.

"Let's go. Grandma Hazel fries the best fish."

Both girls lifted themselves out of their chairs and raced to the cabin, arriving before John.

The smells inviting them indoors were tantalizing and made their mouths water.

The table was set with a platter of fried fish, fried potatoes, and corn on the cob. Fresh-squeezed lemonade was on ice in brightly colored aluminum drinking glasses. It was the picture-perfect summer meal.

"Pass the ketchup, please," Penelope asked. "I want some for my potatoes. Oh, and a little butter for the corn."

Grandma Hazel offered corn-shaped corn holders to those who wanted them. The sisters took two each, stabbed either end of the cob with a holder, and rolled the corn in a combination of butter and a little salt. A corn-and-butter-juice concoction dripped down fingers and hands and chins; it was wiped off and reapplied with each crunchy bite.

The fish were fried to perfection, crispy and seasoned just right. Sunfish bones are small, so everyone was careful. Splitting the fish open, the bulk of the bones were easily taken out. Pulling off the bottom and top fins also disposed of even more bones. The flaky white meat was eaten with fingers so that any remaining bones could be felt with fingertips before placing in mouths. The larger fish fillets were boneless and easy to eat.

Potatoes, crisp on the outside and tender inside, were mixed with sweet Vidalia onions and a little garlic. Grandma Hazel and Penelope liked ketchup on their potatoes; John and CeCe liked them the way they were.

"How about s'mores and a campfire when it gets dark? Girls?" Grandma Hazel grinned, knowing the response.

With shiny faces and sticky hands, CeCe and Penelope looked at each other and said, "Yes!"

"You two even sound alike," said John, shaking his head in disbelief, and took another piece of fish from the platter.

"I'll take that as a compliment," smiled Penelope, throwing her shoulders back and pushing out her chest.

"Me too," mumbled CeCe, mowing through another row of buttery corn.

When dinner was finished and everyone was groaning with extended stomachs, John pushed back his chair and said, "Girls, go play. I'll help Grandma with dishes. Take a little walk and find some sticks for marshmallows. Make mine a good one, long and strong."

"Thanks, Dad. Thanks, Grandma."

"Thanks for supper. It was so good," CeCe complimented the chefs.

"Our pleasure," replied Grandma Hazel, scraping fish bones and empty cobs into the garbage.

Following dinner, the sisters ventured down the dirt road in search of marshmallow sticks and to maybe find an agate or two along the way.

The road had two main tracks, perfect for each girl to follow. The median section was raised, and the dirt wasn't quite packed down as firmly, which revealed patches of grass.

Crouching down to examine a possible agate, Penelope brushed dirt from a beautiful caramel-colored swirly stone the size of a marble. CeCe walked over and turned over the stone in her sister's palm.

"CeCe? I want you to have this rock. You gave me the best rock in the world. And I want you to have this one to remember . . . to remember . . . you know, for when you go back." After an uncomfortable pause, she continued, "I love agates, and I want you to have this one."

In the middle of a lonely dirt road, shaded from the last of the sun's rays, CeCe and Penelope moved toward each other and wrapped their arms around each other in a tight embrace.

"I'll keep it forever," said CeCe, pushing back the flood of tears that were threatening to spill. Pulling back to look Penelope in the eyes, she saw that Penelope's tears were freely flowing. CeCe's eyes were now filled to capacity and soon overflowed their lids too. Several times both girls had to wipe the surge from their cheeks with their fingertips. Smudges and streaks of dirt looked like tribal paint across their faces. The agate may have started their emotional response, but both girls knew that the reason for their tears had to do with the idea of leaving each other.

With a quick squeeze of the shoulders, CeCe tucked her jewel deep into her pocket. "Come on. Let's find those sticks before it gets any darker. John wants the perfect stick, and we don't really know what kind of creatures hang in these woods," she teased. Looking about her, with hands and arms tucked in tight, CeCe mimicked like she was frightened.

"Okay, okay. Let's go, you goofball," Penelope said, wiping one rogue tear from her cheek.

After the four marshmallow sticks were found, the girls peeled back the bark to just the right point and sharpened their sticks. John brought the other supplies to the already blazing campfire.

A bag of marshmallows, a package of chocolate bars, and a box of graham crackers were ready on a small folding table next to John's lawn chair. The four chairs wrapped around half of the fire as the smoke was carried eastward into the woods by a light breeze.

Firewood was stacked off to the side with four large pieces, creating a tepee in the middle of the fire pit. Orange, red, and yellow flames danced in and out and between the logs. It was hard not to stare into the fire with an empty mind; it was hypnotic.

The crinkling of the chocolate bars being opened snapped the silence. Heads turned toward the sound, and smiles broke through as consciousness resurfaced. It was time for s'mores.

The girls speared their marshmallows and stuffed two at a time on their sticks. They debated whether the marshmallows should be browned slowly or lit on fire and charred. It was a split decision, with everyone having a strong opinion. Graham crackers snapped into two sections—a top and bottom—with a section of chocolate placed between. They were ready for the smush of the softened marshmallows.

Eating s'mores proved to be as messy as corn on the cob. Long gooey strings of marshmallow stretched then snapped onto chins. Fingers were glued together and forced apart to place more marshmallows on sticks.

Penelope licked her fingers and became curious about an unheard conversation she was watching between her grandmother and her father. Their eyes had been talking, but they were not verbalizing their thoughts. It was clear that something was going on, and soon enough, she found out.

When everyone had had enough of the sweet treats, the girls and Grandma Hazel laid down their sticks, except for John. He poked at the fire, breaking bottom coals into small pieces resembling gemstones.

"CeCe?" John spoke and then stopped. Looking up at his oldest daughter, he tried again. "CeCe, I wanted to talk to you about when you were little."

"Don't," said CeCe quietly.

"Honey, we need to talk."

"I said don't. I don't want to talk. I definitely don't want to talk here. Not now, maybe not ever." CeCe remained eerily calm for several minutes. Then she exploded. "You have no right!" she screamed. Standing up abruptly, she knocked over her lawn chair and ran to the cabin. The banging screen door was like a gunshot in the dark.

"Dad? What were you thinking? Now she'll never come back!" cried Penelope.

John stood to follow CeCe, but Grandma Hazel placed her hand on his arm. "Sit down, John. She needs to think before she speaks. She will come to you when she's ready."

Penelope turned from the adults and ran to join her sister. Neither of the girls nor John had noticed their three shimmering stars darken under cloud cover.

In the cabin, CeCe was already curled up on one of the two daybeds. She was on her side, face to the wall. Penelope walked in to sit on the other daybed and wait.

CeCe's mind was scattered and traveled between angry questions and accusations and sadness, unexplainable and deeply felt in her heart. She didn't know which feeling was real or right, let alone what she wanted to say. Should she use words to hurt or to heal? Did she know what she wanted? Did she want a father in her life?

After what seemed an eternity, CeCe came to the conclusion that there was one thing she wanted for sure. She knew this without a doubt and with every fiber of her being.

"Penelope? Come sleep over here, okay?"

Without saying a word, Penelope stood, walked to where her sister had shifted onto her back, and pulled back the blanket.

Using the back of her hand to tap her sister's hip, Penelope finally spoke, "Move over, sis."

Chapter Nine

The smell of bacon and freshly brewed coffee drifted into the porch and awakened the girls. They sat up and cuddled under the blanket, straining to hear the hushed tones of a conversation between John and Grandma Hazel. They could only make out a few words. "CeCe ... okay ... all right."

"Whatever happened to your grandpa? The one married to Grandma Hazel?" asked CeCe, deciding the kitchen conversation was unintelligible and one she didn't want to hear.

"They got a divorce when my mom was young. I guess he moved to Alaska or something. I am not really sure. Dad told me I met him once when he visited, but I don't remember—I was two years old or something. So my mom was pretty much raised by Grandma."

Nodding with understanding, CeCe wondered at the similarities between Anna and herself. John and Anna's father seemed to have a lot in common.

Penelope offered more family history. "Dad's mom, Grandma Jean, died right after I was born. So I didn't know her either. But wait, think about it. She knew you.

You were her granddaughter too. Weird! She knew you before she ever knew me. Do you remember her?"

"Nope, but my mom mentioned her once and said she was pretty sick and had to stay in bed. She really liked Grandpa Arnie though," CeCe finished.

"He is so sweet and nice. Dad looks a lot like him. It's fun when we go to his farm to visit. We have a ton of cousins and family all around his place. But uh, they must have known you too, right? Why didn't Grandpa or Uncle Stanley or Auntie Lou tell me I had a sister? Why didn't they tell Dad to go get you? I just don't get it," stammered Penelope. "It's just wrong."

"I hadn't thought about that, but you're right. I'm not so happy with the adults in our lives at the moment. I have a ton of questions that I want answered." CeCe drifted in her own thinking then added in haste, "But not today."

Grandma Hazel announced her entrance onto the porch, "Gooood morning. I thought I heard some chitchatting out here. Are you ready for some breakfast?" A hand was placed under each girl's chin; she tilted their heads upward to look into both pairs of eyes. "How are you two doing?" Eyebrows raised, she grinned and waited.

"Yeah, we're fine, Grandma. Right, CeCe?"

"Penelope's right. We are fine, thanks. The bacon smells great."

After kissing each girl's forehead, Grandma Hazel tossed the brown cotton blanket aside, and the three walked into the dining room.

"Good morning, girls," said John rather sheepishly. He ruffled the hair on each of their heads when he rose to refill his cobalt-blue coffee cup. Nothing about the previous night's near argument and the issues it brought up were mentioned. He had placed them on a shelf in the hopes that they could one day be brought down and discussed.

"Did you pick these, Grandma?" Penelope asked, popping three large raspberries into her mouth.

"Yes, I did, honey. I picked three pints the other day, and this is what's left," she said, pointing to a small bowl of sweet yet tangy fruit.

Using her fingers to put two pieces of bacon on her plate, and picking up another slice to be eaten immediately, CeCe said, "I don't think I've ever eaten so much."

Penelope and John nodded, but with full mouths, they couldn't speak their agreement.

Plates full of buttered wheat toast, hickory-smoked bacon, scrambled eggs, and handpicked raspberries filled the table. Milk and orange juice left mustaches on upper lips.

"We'll do dishes this morning," offered Penelope. Her grandmother had already washed the frying pans from both the bacon and the eggs.

"Fair enough. I gladly accept your offer," said Grandma. "That will give me time to pick a few more raspberries for you to take back to town."

"Hey, CeCe, sorry. I forgot to ask if you wanted to do dishes," laughed Penelope.

"It would be my honor." CeCe nodded toward Grandma Hazel. "But you get to wash."

Washing and drying dishes took longer than expected. The girls talked and turned the work into a bit of playtime. Penelope shaped soapsuds into swirling patterns on plates, and CeCe would blow the soapy patterns back off the plates and into the water and, sometimes, the floor.

Grandma pulled the veil back on her wide-brimmed hat and returned with freshly picked raspberries. She cleaned and packaged two pints for the girls to take home and made a recommendation that they be placed on some ice cream a little later. CeCe and Penelope thought that was a great idea.

John loaded the car and started the good-bye process. Everyone received a squeeze, kiss, and bit of advice from Grandma Hazel before getting into the vehicle. "John, take your time and don't rush. Love you. Penelope, take care of your family and don't judge either of them. Love you. CeCe, when you're ready to talk, speak honestly and without anger. Love you."

"I love you, Hazel. Thank you."

"I love you, Grandma. Thanks."

"I love you, Grandma Hazel. I hope I get to visit again really soon."

Looking through the back window of the car, both girls and Grandma Hazel waved until neither could see the other. "I always feel sad leaving here. It's the same when I leave Grandpa Arnie. It is kind of a lonely feeling."

"I know what you mean. I really love her. It feels like she is my grandma too," said CeCe.

"I'll share her with you," Penelope said, taking hold of her sister's hand and giving it a little squeeze.

*   *   *

Upon arriving home, the girls unpacked and decided that a mellow day in the house had been earned. They wanted to make chocolate chip cookies, watch TV, and just plain take it easy.

John threw a load of clothes into the washing machine and decided that the lawn needed mowing and a little trim again. "If you need me, I will be outside. Have fun and do not do anything I wouldn't do."

After her dad left, Penelope asked her sister, "Why do adults always say that? What kind of trouble does he think we could get into with him just outside?"

"I don't know. I don't get adults—at all," CeCe said, stressing the last two words.

"Let's start these cookies, and we can watch TV at the same time," said Penelope, pulling a bag of chocolate chips from the cupboard.

"Got it! Where's the recipe?"

"My favorite is the one on the back of the bag. See here?"

"Okay, let's get everything we need. I will get the eggs and flour and sugar," offered CeCe.

The girls opened and closed cabinet doors and drawers until all the necessary tools and ingredients were placed on the counter. It was a cooperative affair, with each girl measuring an item, the other placing it in the large stainless steel bowl. After Penelope mixed all the dry ingredients, CeCe was ready with eggs, butter, and vanilla extract.

The most important and featured item was added last—chocolate chips. Neither girl resisted the urge to sample a few just to make sure they tasted right.

"Ugh, this batter is sooooo thick. It's hard to mix," moaned Penelope, handing the large spoon to her sister. "Your turn."

CeCe mixed and stirred while Penelope preheated the oven to 350 and set out a darkened cookie sheet. When the batter was ready, both girls tasted it.

"Perfect," said CeCe.

The sisters moved quickly by placing two-inch blobs of cookie dough on the cookie sheet. A dozen cookies at a time could be baked, and Penelope placed the first batch in the oven. CeCe set the timer for twelve minutes and moved to the living room to watch TV until the next batch was ready.

"What do you want to watch?"

"Hmm," said CeCe, clicking through the channels. There were only a few, and most channels had programming only adults would like.

"Well, let's laugh. Is there a cartoon with sisters?"

Kneeling next to CeCe, Penelope laughed and gave her sister a little shoulder bump. Exaggerating her actions, CeCe pretended that the bump had been a shove and tipped over. Her mouth was rounded and eyes were shocked.

"You are funny," laughed Penelope.

"No, you are," said CeCe right back.

Their laughter was switched off by the buzzing of the kitchen timer.

"Oh, good. Come on, the cookies are done," said CeCe, jumping up from the floor.

The smells from the kitchen were like hugs from Grandma Hazel. They were warm and inviting and made you want more. Using two red striped potholders, CeCe pulled the cookies from the oven and set them on the stove top. A large sheet of waxed paper was placed on the end of the counter, and Penelope used a metal-slotted spatula to transfer cookies from the hot metal to the opaque paper to cool. The rows of cookies were perfect.

When the first batch had been situated comfortably, another dozen two-inch scoops were placed on the now cooled cookie sheet and carefully slid onto the middle rack in the oven.

"We had better try them," Penelope suggested, already holding one of the warm treats in her hand.

CeCe saw no reason to argue with this line of thinking and used her thumb and pointer finger to test the warmth of the cookie she was going to devour. Her mouth watered as she took a bite of the melty goodness.

Together the girls agreed, "Mmmm."

The cookies were slightly crisp on the edges and tender in the middle. The warm chocolate covered their fingertips, so both sisters chose to clean them with their mouths.

"Perfect. We are fabulous bakers," said Penelope. "Hey, let's go watch TV. Grab another cookie."

The Disney movie *The Parent Trap* was found. "Yes, I knew there would be one that had sisters in it. In fact, it is a little like our story, only we don't go to camp, and I don't think our parents are going to get back together."

"I think you're right. I love this movie though. I saw it a year ago in the theater. This will be great."

Draping herself on the couch, each girl found her nest and settled in to watch.

Music and title credits announced the beginning of the movie. "It's about time," sighed CeCe.

* * *

A puzzled look emerged from behind glazed eyes. CeCe's nose wrinkled, and she turned toward Penelope.

Awareness slapped both girls at the same time, "The cookies!"

CeCe jumped from the couch, ran into the kitchen, and grabbed the potholders, pulling a dozen forgotten dark crisps from the oven. Penelope was whipping a dishtowel in the air as if in surrender, trying to erase the smelly haze from the air before the smoke drifted and screamed for Dad.

"Oh my gosh," chuckled Penelope in low, hushed tones. She stopped waving the towel and waited to see if she had accomplished her task. John didn't show up asking questions. She was successful.

"I can't believe we forgot the cookies. We totally didn't set the timer," CeCe said in a nervous laugh.

"Um, maybe we should pay closer attention to the next batch? We can watch the movie *after* the cookies," recommended Penelope.

Scraping hockey pucks into the garbage bag, CeCe had to use a bit of muscle to get the baked-on remains entirely off the cookie sheet. The stench still lingered. The girls reloaded the cookie sheet with another array of dough, adding to the few cookies that remained from the first batch. They were absolute in their decision to sit at the kitchen table and play cards.

Four dozen minus six cookies later, the girls cleaned their mess and tenderly placed their creations into the black-and-white cow cookie jar on the counter.

"Let's watch TV later when it's dark outside," said CeCe.

"Good idea. Hey, let's pack up some munchies and head to our fort in the woods," Penelope excitedly responded.

"I'm right with you."

CeCe opened a drawer to retrieve a small paper bag while Penelope gathered two cookies in a paper towel, a small stack of soda crackers, and two chunks of cheese. A thermos of ice water was readied, and a few garden tools were grabbed from the shed, just in case the fort needed remodeling.

The sunny heat of the afternoon brought about beads of sweat on the foreheads of the girls as they raced their bikes to the entrance of the cool, damp woods.

The steep but short drop marked the starting gate of the path into the dark. Immediately, it felt as if icy arms wrapped them. Shivers ran up and down their necks and backs as their bikes slowed to watch the rough and rocky path before them.

The girls set their kickstands and unloaded the tools and supplies when they arrived at their forested dwelling. The former homestead hadn't changed, and the brick table and chairs were exactly as they had left them the previous week. The fort was still theirs and theirs alone. All it needed was a few finishing touches.

Penelope chose the handheld garden hoe and handed the trowel to CeCe. Without a plan, yet fully aware that any effort would enhance their fort, the girls went to work. Half-buried bricks were brought to the surface, cleaned, and stacked for later use. Leaves layered by the seasons sounded sloppy as they were cleared to expose long-forgotten dirt underneath. And bugs hidden by the bricks, leaves, and rocks were rendered as specimens to be examined by their excavators.

Following a particularly close inspection of a rather large beetle, CeCe spoke, "I love that he's so shiny. Bugs don't bother me, but I hate—I mean I really hate—spiders. If we see one, you'll have to deal with it, okay?"

"I'll save you from the big bad spiders, sis. Don't worry. But you are in charge of mice for me."

"Got your back."

The hard work was paying off. Rooms known only to the designers began to take shape. The home now had a kitchen complete with table and chairs, a storage area for future hidden treasures, and a proper entrance marked with large rocks and tall branches.

Sitting at the kitchen table, eating cookies first, the girls proudly looked around at their handiwork.

"We should make a time capsule and bury it here. At school, we made one in the second grade. At the beginning of the year, we put in stuff about us and wrapped it. Then we opened it at the end of the year. That would be fun," said CeCe, reaching for some cheese.

"I love it. What do you think we should put in it?" Seeing her sister's decision to continue with the snacks, Penelope joined her. "Hey, you know what this means?"

"What?"

"That you will have to come back. You can't make a time capsule and then forget about it forever, you know. You have to come back to open it. If that's the case, I will absolutely do it."

CeCe's emotions felt like they were walking on a tightrope. Fear was wobbly. She was unsure what to say to her sister. It was important to say the right thing, but what that was, she didn't know. Looking at her waiting sibling, CeCe decided to talk around the discussion. "It would be so fun to make a time capsule with you. What would you put in it?"

The distraction of a question worked this time, but CeCe knew she would have to deal with the issue sooner or later.

"Let's put in pictures of us. Oh, and Dad's. Maybe pictures of our moms should be in there, too. How about some new rocks? We could find some agates together and put them in." Penelope thought hard about additional possibilities.

Relieved, CeCe added, "Let's have some crackers with our cheese."

After their break, the girls went back to work, switching tools. Dirt accumulated under fingernails, on knees, and even on faces. Neither girl noticed or would have cared. They were in their safe sister world, where unanswered questions were secure and where time slowed for those that needed it to. However, upon leaving the woods, those minutes would become nasty and cruel, and the real world would soon expect answers.

The ride home was slow and quiet. The day was hot, and the girls were in no hurry to wash away the soil from their homeland.

"I know you aren't sure about coming back yet, but I just want you to know that I really want you to visit again. I won't bug you about it though. I love you, CeCe."

It was as if Penelope could hear CeCe's fear loud and clear. She could only imagine the thoughts that must be running through CeCe's head.

It was CeCe, not her fear, who chose to speak to her sister. "I love you too, Penelope."

*   *   *

Dinner with John was more quiet than usual, until dessert. Two chocolate chip cookies looking like ears on a mound of chocolate ice cream were placed in front of each child. Then John spooned raspberries onto the structure, as recommended by Grandma Hazel.

"The cookies are the best, girls. Nice job. What else did you do this afternoon?"

"We have the coolest fort in the woods, Dad. Do you have some old stuff, like blankets or chairs that we can have? Oh, and we need a big jar or something that we can use for a time capsule. Maybe some duct tape too."

"Uh, huh. That sounds interesting. I'll look around and see what I can find. Don't take things unless you ask though. If I remember correctly, the last time you wanted stuff from the house, we ran out of silverware," John teased but winked at both Penelope and CeCe.

The mention of missing silverware brought up shared stories of past wrongdoings, and soon the family of three was laughing loudly at themselves and each other. After kitchen cleanup, the girls resumed their positions on the couch, and John relaxed in the recliner while he routinely rested his eyes during TV time.

Two hours later, the girls left John to continue resting and went outside to sit on the steps. They knew all too well that after this evening, they would only have one full day left. Two nights and CeCe's questions would have to be answered and decisions made.

Leaning against the wrought-iron railing, each girl sat on a step, with the younger of the two sisters seated on the lowest one.

"Hey, CeCe, look. Fireflies."

"Where?"

Penelope pointed toward the green leaves of the lilac bushes at the edge of the yard. "I think they are so cool. Sometimes out my bedroom window, I watch them for hours, but I'm always alone. Now when I'll see them, I will think of you."

"Did you know that the Mayan Indians in Mexico thought that the firefly was connected to the stars?" asked CeCe.

"Wow! How did you know that?"

"I did research on them in school. They were said to be the messengers to the Mayan gods. Also, they like the star apple trees in the Philippines. I don't remember, but there is a long story about that. And if two fireflies enter your house, it is considered good luck." CeCe gazed past the moving lights and tried to remember more of what she had written.

"Maybe we could open the door to let two inside." Penelope smiled. "The star thing is the best though. It's kind of like our stars, you know, the three we saw with Dad. The fireflies must be reminding us of our stars, or maybe they will take messages to our stars. I like that idea."

"Me too. How about when I go home and see a firefly, I'll give it a message to give to our stars, and you'll be able to hear it and see it? You could do the same to me," CeCe said softly.

"I promise I won't forget, CeCe. Close your eyes. Let's make this the most special memory of all."

John awakened to find the girls outside. He stood at the doorway, arms crossed, and wondered why they sat so quietly with closed eyes. He was unaware of the wishes and prayers being sent to stars and fireflies in the hopes that memories could always be recalled and that two little girls would each always have her sister by her side.

Chapter Ten

The alarm clock on the maple nightstand next to Penelope's side of the bed had been set for 7:00 a.m. on the morning of their last full day. Albert Einstein eyed and waited without judgment from his poster position until finally, after three pushes on the snooze alarm, the girls stretched and turned to face each other. They were snuggled and cozy under the blanket, and the fan that blew toward them at medium speed occasionally tossed small hairs onto CeCe's forehead. Brushing the imaginary spider from her temple, CeCe said, "Good morning."

"Good morning. I can't believe that this is our last full day. I want to do so much. I don't even know where we should start. What do we do first? We've crossed a ton off our list, but there is so much more to do. We only have one day and a wake-up left."

CeCe truly didn't know what they should do. She was unsure of what to say. The love she felt for her sister was strong, and never would she want her words to be cruel or to cause injury. Penelope wasn't as subtle as she thought about her questioning concerning the day, and CeCe knew that she wanted the commitment of a return visit in order to complete all they wanted to accomplish—more importantly, to grow up as sisters beyond this one brief encounter.

"A wake-up?"

"Yeah," said Penelope. "You know. When we wake up it will be the last day, not a full day. All we have to do is wake up."

"Oh"—that was all that CeCe could muster. Tomorrow. How do you possibly say good-bye to someone who means the world to you? How had her father managed to do this to her, to both of them? CeCe had always defined herself by her father's absence and not his presence. She had suffered through Dad's Day at school, the unknown branches of her family tree, and the grasp that abandonment had on her heart. After all the years of safety nets being embedded into her thoughts and soul, he had managed to untie a few strings, and now she felt a weakening of her surety and stubbornness. But was the diminishing anger because of her sister, her father, or both? Regardless of the need to talk about her feelings, pride ate her ability to speak and made her quiet.

CeCe's shoulders jumped toward her ears, and she smiled at her sister.

"Well, we could start by spoiling ourselves. Let's paint our nails. I have a basket with tons of colors. Hey, we should paint each nail a different color," suggested Penelope.

"Let's do it," CeCe said, bolting upright and pulling her right foot toward her to examine the possibilities. She was happy for the distraction.

Taking a blue wicker basket from a shelf in the closet, Penelope and CeCe emptied the contents onto their bed. Emery boards, pink toe separators, and a rainbow of colored bottles were placed on display. Neither girl chose to remove the remnants of past pedicures from their nails; they painted over the old with new and bright.

"I'm picking this turquoise for my big toes," said CeCe, twisting the top of her color preference.

"Okay, I'll wait until you're done. I want mine to be the same," Penelope said, nodding in agreement with her sister's choice.

Turquoise, hot pink, glittering purple, bright orange, and sky blue were smoothed onto each nail as the pink toe separators prevented the dancing colors from bumping into each other.

Sweet and buttery waffle smells waved upward from the kitchen and halted their deep discussion of whether to continue with their short fingernails or not. Walking on their heels, toes aimed at the ceiling, the girls took longer than normal to descend the stairs for breakfast.

"Ah, I thought you two might like to start your day with one of my specialties," said John, looking at his daughters who had quietly slipped into their spots at the table.

A plateful of warm lightly browned waffles sat waiting for toppings. Butter, maple syrup, a bowl of ripe strawberries, and a Cool Whip container were the options.

Splitting her waffle into two sections, Penelope smeared butter over the square holes and let it melt into the little pockets. A light coating of syrup was zigzagged over the top and swirled with the butter for a savory yet sweet combination. The remaining half held fruity juices and chunks of strawberries with a dollop of whipped cream. For the second time that morning, the girls decided to be alike. CeCe followed Penelope's lead and prepared her waffles in an identical manner.

"I can never decide, so I do both."

"Me either. This looks great, John."

"Yeah, thanks, Dad. You are the best waffle maker."

"The finest. Never to be surpassed," boasted John. "Eat up before they get cold."

Not waiting to be told twice, the girls slid their forks through the layers to create bursts of flavor for each bite taken. Cold milk extinguished sweetness when it became overwhelming. CeCe again followed Penelope's lead by also using her middle finger to clear any of the remaining goo from her plate.

With a final lick of the syrupy mixture, Penelope asked, "Dad? Remember to find something for a time capsule today, and we want to have a lemonade stand. Do we have all the stuff?"

"I will find a container for the time capsule. Consider it done. What do you plan to do with all your profits from selling lemonade? I better get a cut." John finished his breakfast and stood to separate the last waffle from its maker's hold.

"I don't know. Maybe candy. Maybe nail polish. It depends how much we make. We'll share our treats with you though."

"I'm not so sure I need nail polish," John said while holding out his fingernails for the girls to appreciate. "Everything you need is in the lower right-hand cupboard."

"Yes," exclaimed Penelope. Grabbing her sister's hand, the girls hobbled back upstairs to ready themselves for the day.

*   *   *

A yellow plastic pitcher was set on the countertop, and clear plastic cups were pulled from their hiding place deep inside the bottom cupboard. Using the back of the powdered lemonade container, they found and made the recipe for lemonade perfection.

"Oh my gosh, we need a sign! And what are we going to use for a table?" asked CeCe.

"Mmmm, we can use my wagon so then we can move it if we need to. I'll get some paper and markers."

...red the dissolving powder with a long-handled wooden spoon until it completely merged with the cold water, forming a spinning vortex in the center of the pitcher. Ice cubes twisted from their holding position in the tray and were dropped with a plop into the tangy liquid.

Penelope returned with the sign supplies, sat on her bent right leg, and stared at the blank paper. "How much should we charge?"

"How about one dollar a glass? Is that too much?"

"Well, we should get at least five glasses out of the pitcher. It would be perfect if we could get five bucks. We could get candy and something else. A dollar might be too much though. How about fifty cents?" Using a black marker, Penelope wrote the words "Lemonade: 50¢ a glass." Using a pencil first, she added her best freehand drawing of a lemon. A bright yellow marker added the necessary eye-catching touch.

CeCe added, "I love the sign. We could call it 'P & C's Lemonade.' It sounds like a real store name, doesn't it?"

"Yeah, the P & C fits right here," said Penelope, pointing to a corner above the large bubble letters of lemonade. After making the changes, Penelope added,

"Meet me out front with the lemonade, and I'll get my wagon from the garage."

While preparing the wagon, John offered the girls their first sale of the day. "Here's my money. I'm ready for some of that famous P & C Lemonade. Do I get a discount?"

Penelope collected the correct change from her father while CeCe poured. "No discounts, Dad. We need our money."

Drinking the entire amount in two large swallows, John laughed, "That was wonderful. Now I have an errand to run. You girls be good. Have fun."

After loading the wagon, the girls decided that the corner of Main and Third Street was the ideal location for a lemonade stand. It was normally a busy intersection and provided a sidewalk for the wagon and a curb upon which to sit.

The first thirty minutes of waiting for the lines of customers to appear was exciting and full of potential. Horns honked, and passengers waved; the business owners returned the enthusiasm with waves of their own. But no one stopped to quench his or her thirst.

The heat of the day dropped onto the heads of the young entrepreneurs, causing dehydration and boredom.

"I'm thirsty," said Penelope. "Do you think we should share just one glass? It will only be one, plus it looks so good."

"I was thinking the same thing."

Moving together, Penelope held the glass while CeCe poured, then she offered the first drink to her sister, who took it without argument.

"That was great. Here, your turn."

Penelope drank, wiped the lemonade off her upper lip, and handed the glass back to CeCe.

When the glass was empty, the girls sat again on the curb to wait. Penelope set her chin in her hands, which were supported by her knees. CeCe was stretched back, using her hands to prop her up from behind.

At the same time, both girls came to attention. Penelope popped up, and CeCe sprang forward. Two prospective customers were walking on the sidewalk, right toward the P & C Lemonade Stand. The two women were walking at a steady pace, and each was pushing a baby stroller. They were talking to each other when it became apparent that they had shared a mutual joke and laughed.

CeCe and Penelope stood as professionals by the wagon. Eyes met from the closing distance, but the girls waited until the women were next to them before they spoke.

"Would either of you like to buy a glass of cold lemonade?" asked CeCe.

"It's only fifty cents, and it is really refreshing," added the blond salesperson.

"Only two little quarters, huh? I guess we should take two," said the closer of the two women. She pulled her wallet out of a diaper bag, opened it, and handed a dollar bill to Penelope.

CeCe grinned at Penelope as she set out two plastic cups and filled them with the sparkling liquid. The ice no longer resembled cubes but small slivers. However, the glasses were cold, and condensation formed quickly on their plastic exteriors. CeCe handed one to each customer. "Thanks for your business," she said while Penelope tucked the money in her pocket.

"You're welcome," both women said at the same time.

"Thanks for buying, sis," said the taller of the two women.

"Are you two sisters?" asked Penelope.

"Yes, we are sisters. Are you two sisters?" asked the second of the two women.

"Yes!" said CeCe and Penelope.

"Of course you are. I can see that you two look so much alike. I'm Samantha, and this is my sister Sarah."

"We think we look alike too," said CeCe. She wrapped her arm around Penelope and gave it a big squeeze. "It is nice to meet both of you."

After taking a long drink, Samantha bent to talk to the toddler in her stroller. The little girl was wearing a pink ruffled bonnet with a floral sundress. Helping her child, Samantha let the little girl drink from her lemonade. Drool mixed with the tang of lemon spilled onto the child's chin and dress front, and her chubby hands grabbed both sides of the glass. Laughing, the mother remained in control but let her daughter spill a little more. The sogginess and the child transfixed her grinning mother. It was as if she had completed the most amazing magic trick, one that no one else had ever performed.

The spell broke when the plastic cup was squeezed just a little too tightly. It buckled in the middle, and a lemon splash kissed the toddler's nose. Surprise on the faces of her audience was replaced by laughter.

Pulling a wet wipe from a pastel-striped diaper bag attached to the back of the stroller, Samantha very gently erased the stickiness from her daughter's face.

"Thanks for the lemonade, girls," she said. She handed the empty cups, complete with the now sticky wet wipe, to Penelope for her disposal.

"Thanks," replied the younger sisters.

The women pushed off and continued their stroll down the sidewalk.

"She was so cute," cooed CeCe.

"I know. Plus we made one dollar."

"I love that they think we look alike. I thought we did, but it is nice to know others think so too," said CeCe.

"Sisters forever!" Penelope smiled.

*   *   *

Ten short minutes of additional waiting and the girls found themselves bored once again.

"Okay, I'm thirsty. Let's have another drink," said Penelope.

CeCe pulled the glass they had used prior and started pouring the lemonade. This time it was Penelope who took the first drink then offered it to her older sister.

"You know, there is only a little left. I don't think there is enough for a whole glass. Maybe we should drink that too," suggested CeCe.

"Yeah, plus I want to go spend our money. Let's close up shop and head to the store."

Draining the last of the lemonade, the girls made their way two blocks west to Anderson's Gift Shop. They parked the wagon outside the door and entered with the intention to spend every dime of their hard-earned $1.50.

The decision to spend their money was a serious one. Every aisle was scrutinized for sale or specialty items that might fall into their price range. The few toys that were actually in the store were either too costly or uninteresting. However, a small bag of miscellaneous paper tattoos was placed on the possibility list. The candy aisle seemed their greatest source of interest as the girls now had more choices.

When the decisions were finally made, the girls had a bag of orange circus peanuts, two small packages of orange fruits, a Salted Nut Roll, one KitKat, and a small bag of peace sign tattoos.

The sisters immediately went to the restroom after making their purchases. They opened their bag of tattoos and chose matching blue peace signs the size of a quarter. Wetting their right forearms, they placed the tattoos face side down and applied pressure for the recommended thirty seconds. When the time was right, the girls carefully peeled off the paper backing, revealing two perfectly circular blue peace signs impressed on their skin.

"I love it," said Penelope. Extending her arm outward, she turned it from side to side, examining her newly acquired blue blemish.

"Me too," said CeCe. "Peace signs are so cool, and now we have the same one. I hope it lasts for a long time. Maybe we should be careful when we wash our arms, or maybe, just maybe, we shouldn't even wash them."

Laughing, the sisters left the bathroom.

It was time to head home.

"While Dad is making lunch, let's climb my favorite tree. Oh, and bring the candy. It will be the best place to eat it," Penelope suggested when they had returned home.

Penelope's favorite climbing tree was located in the neighbor's yard, right on the backyard border between the two lawns. The neighbor, Mr. Harwood, was the postman, and he knew everyone in town. He never minded when Penelope climbed. He knew that she was respectful of his tree and his lawn.

The large maple had the ideal crook upon which to place your foot for the first pull upward. Penelope led the way, showing her sister the handholds that would be both safe and efficient. Halfway up the massive trunk was a perfect recliner of a branch that was attached at a 90 degree angle. It was wide enough to scoot across until seated in the saddle of the limb. The girls dangled their legs and looked through leaves at their surroundings, as if they were in the bird's nest of a tall ship.

Opening the circus peanuts, Penelope said, "In the fall, I love to come up here. The leaves make everything look red, even my arms. It is so pretty and quiet. One time though, when I put my foot in that first cross area, there was dog poop on it. I was so grossed out. Then it made me wonder who else climbs my tree. I still don't know because I have never seen anyone else up here."

"Oooooh, gross. When did that happen?" CeCe looked down from her perch to where she had just come from, pausing after taking the first of two bites from the orange candy.

Laughing, Penelope said, "That was a long time ago. It was over a year, at least. There is no poop left, don't worry. But I check every time."

Most of the candy was eaten, and wrappers were put back into the bag.

"Let's make the time capsule after lunch," said Penelope.

"What should we put in it?" asked CeCe.

"How about two of the tattoos from the extras we have? And we could put in two rocks."

"Yeah, and let's write a letter. It will be fun to read when we are old."

Again. It had happened again. The pause that followed was thick, but CeCe could feel her doubts about seeing her sister in the future topple like a line of closely placed dominos.

She looked directly into Penelope's eyes and didn't waver this time when she spoke. "Penelope, when I said that we would open our time capsule when we are older, I meant it. You are my sister—heck, you are my only and best sister. We will be family forever, and I will always want to see you and spend time with you. I will see you again. I don't know when, but I will make sure it happens."

Penelope stopped mid bite when she saw the seriousness painted on her sister's face. Her words scooped buckets of tears from her eyes. CeCe's facial features became distorted and swimmy, and Penelope's throat was tight with restraint. Finding her balance in the treetop, Penelope allowed her arms to encircle CeCe's neck. She couldn't speak words that anyone would have understood, but her laughter through tears was able to express the relief and joy she was feeling.

CeCe tucked her face into Penelope's shoulder and freed her own tears that had been held captive for so long. She too was relieved that one decision about her future family had been finalized. Nothing that she could envision would ever let her be separated for any length of time from her sister. It was comforting to be absolute.

"Girls, lunch!"

The soggy moment melted when John made his announcement from the back door.

Pulling away, the girls steadied themselves and their hearts.

"Forever and always, CeCe, you said. Pinky-swear with me that we are sisters forever and always."

Cradled in the arms of the tree, the girls hooked their smallest fingers around the other's and verbalized to the universe their promise.

"I swear, Penelope. Forever and always."

"I swear, CeCe. Forever and always."

"Girls, lunch!"

"Coming, Dad," yelled Penelope. Looking toward her sister, she added, "I don't think I have ever been this happy. I was so scared, but not anymore. Thank you."

"I love you, Penelope. I was scared too, but not anymore, at least not about you," CeCe spoke honestly.

"I know."

"Let's get down and get lunch, or John will come up to get us," laughed CeCe.

Helping each other climb down from their perch, CeCe carried the brown bag of candy and wrappers. The girls skipped the short distance home.

*   *   *

"Hey, you two, tell me all about the lemonade stand. How much did you make? How much candy do I get?"

CeCe awkwardly handed John the paper bag of goodies and trash. Her earlier openness with her sister had peeled back emotional layers like an onion, but when it came to John, her anger, confusion, and even shame for her lack of sincerity felt like tinfoil on a tooth filling.

Peeking inside the bag, John said, "Garbage? You saved me the trash?"

"Dig, Dad. We left you some orange fruit and a KitKat if you want them."

"Nah, you two earned it. You eat it. You two do need to eat something a bit healthier though. Go wash up. The tacos will be on the table when you get back."

"Sounds great, Dad."

CeCe followed her sister without so much as a glance at John.

*   *   *

The family of three filled hard-shell tacos with seasoned meat, cheddar cheese, tomatoes, lettuce, and mild taco sauce. Using two hands still couldn't help to control the contents inside the shell from plunging back onto the plate. Even more pieces were lost when crunchy bites were taken from the ends. The plates were soon covered with leftovers that were eaten with forks.

Mostly, Penelope shared the brief but important story of P & C's Lemonade Stand. She revealed everything, even their thirst and drinking of the profits. CeCe offered agreement when needed and added an occasional word or two.

Penelope was unaware of the quiet descending on her sister. She was still spinning in her delight over her knowledge of CeCe's promise.

John noticed.

He didn't say anything about the tear trails and puffy eyes rimmed with red. It was obvious that something momentous had taken place. He would love to know what had happened but knew better than to say anything. He desperately needed to talk to CeCe, and time was quickly becoming a larger and meaner monster. His oldest daughter would be leaving tomorrow, and he would need to talk to her in person. A phone call was unacceptable. Her face, her eyes, her body language had to be seen. He needed her to see him as well.

It was obvious that something was floating around CeCe's brain. He sensed her mix of emotions. Was what she had to say something that would ignite bliss within him or slam him with sorrow deeper than when he had lost her the first time? Trusting that when it was time to talk, he would find the words, he wondered instead when and where their meeting should take place.

"Dad? Dad? Did you hear me?"

Pulled back from his distracted thinking, John stumbled on his response, "Uh, yeah, I was just thinking about doing the dishes and what I should make for supper."

"Well, I was saying that we need the container for the time capsule. Did you have time to find one?"

"I did. It is clean and on the end table in the living room with a roll of clear strapping tape. That should work better than even duct tape because you can mostly see right through it."

Jumping up from the table, Penelope leaned over the back of her father and kissed him on the cheek. "Thanks, Dad. I love you."

"I love you too, baby." John's arms reached back, pulling his daughter's face closer so he could give her a kiss and a squeeze.

Once again, John and CeCe's eyes met. However, this time they held a little longer because each knew the time was coming when doors would be opened. Neither knew what key would unlock that door, but it would happen soon.

*   *   *

Gathered items for the time capsule were placed on the living room floor. CeCe and Penelope arranged and rearranged to ensure that they had everything: two peace sign tattoos, two rocks from outside the house, and the recipe off the back of a full bag of chocolate chips. The chips were then placed in an olive-colored

Tupperware bowl. Two unread letters were written, folded, and placed into envelopes.

The large plastic container featured a metal lid that would help seal and preserve the treasures in its tomb. Stickers, markers, and pictures drawn by two young artists decorated the capsule.

"Hey, let's add important words on paper, cut them out, and glue them on. What words should we use?" asked Penelope.

"Our names, of course. Oh, and how about words about the stuff we have done, like *swimming*, *tree*, and *lemonade*."

"Yeah, we should have *fishing*, *cookies*, and *fireworks*. And we can't forget *stars*. And we can draw a picture of every word."

With bent heads, the sisters went to work. They talked about each activity as they wrote and drew. The words gave them a way in which to remember. Occasionally, a sort of melancholy would chip away at their happiness, and they would become quiet and linger on a letter, as if riding on their memories. The mood was never gloomy, but heaviness was beginning to settle in—and both girls knew why.

The front door slammed and startled the girls, causing both to flinch. Their heads turned toward the sound. John entered the kitchen with his hands behind his back.

"You scared us, Dad. What do you have there? What are you hiding?" Penelope asked.

"Well, I was going to save this for tomorrow, but seeing as how you two are working on such an important job, I thought you might let me add one thing to your time capsule."

"Sure, that's okay with you, right, CeCe?" asked Penelope.

"Yeah, what is it?"

Pulling a white bag from behind his back, John dangled the bag like bait on a hook. It was twisted in such a way that the store couldn't be identified. "Maybe I should wait."

"Nooooo," Penelope and CeCe sang in chorus.

"Well, I had this gift made for all three of us. Then I figured I should get one extra, just for the capsule. It is not expensive, and it is not fancy. However, it is pretty cool. Actually, they turned out—"

"Daaaad, just show us," whined Penelope.

John started to untwist the bag; he placed his hand inside and said, "As I was saying. They turned out really—"

Now it was time for both girls to whine; they repeated, "Noooooo!"

John pulled his hand out of the bag and used his fingers to comb back his blond hair. He stretched the reveal just a few seconds longer. Finally, he placed his hand back into the bag and pulled out a four-by-six picture frame. It was a simple glossy black frame and had no adornment. The beauty of the gift was behind the frame's glass and stared out at the trio. The picture was the one that had been taken of them on the Fourth of July. The one that had been taken by the kind lady who had offered her help. The one that had been taken while they were having a picnic under the tree. It was a picture of John, Penelope, and CeCe.

All three were quiet as John brought out two more identical frames holding their family of three. He presented each girl with her own frame and held one for himself. Lastly, he removed a single copy of the picture. This one was not in a frame but on its own. "I thought this one could be put in your time capsule since we each have our own copy. I was going to give it to Grandma Hazel, but I'll get her another copy." Not wanting to rush or push the moment, John stopped to wait for his daughter's responses.

"Oh my gosh, Dad. This is the best present ever. I love it. We all look great. I am so happy you did this." Penelope kept repeating words, shaking her head in admiration and surprise, and gave her dad a bear hug complete with a grunt.

CeCe, on the other hand, stared into the faces of the people looking back at her. She could see happiness, but she also remembered her feelings of that day—so much confusion and so many questions. Most of those questions were still present. She also remembered the first picture given to her by John and Penelope. It had been of a family of two. The new picture held three family members. Looking at the three of them, she could also feel her heart start to weaken. She never would have guessed, even two months ago, that she would be looking into John's face, let alone her sister's. She never would have thought that she could feel such utter and complete love for her sister. Yet here she was in a kitchen, holding a framed picture of the three of them. She realized at that moment that she had John's nose.

"Thanks, John. It really is wonderful. I love it" was all she could rally for now.

It was CeCe's turn to notice that John's eyes were red rimmed and a bit puffy. *I wonder if he's been crying*, she thought to herself. For a moment, she felt like reaching out to him, but she was scared—and the feeling passed.

John had indeed been crying. Earlier, while removing the pictures from the order envelope, his breath caught between a gasp and a sob. Only John could know how much he loved his two girls. He thought that maybe all pairs of eyes looking at the photographer had a bit of sadness at the edges. The picture spoke of all the unsaid words hanging in the air like the leaves of that tree they sat under. It was the first time he really saw the resemblance between Penelope and CeCe, which meant they also looked like him. He smiled at that thought.

"This picture makes our time capsule perfect. Now, if it gets opened two hundred years from now, people will know what we looked like. I love that idea," said Penelope.

"Two hundred years from now? Hmm, I am thinking they will wonder who that handsome man with those goofy girls is," teased John.

"CeCe, will you put the picture in the capsule? I have to color my last word for the outside."

John and CeCe's hands met halfway as the picture was exchanged from one to the other. "Thanks. John. I . . . forget it," said CeCe.

"Yes?" John questioned with too much intensity.

"Nothing. Just forget it." CeCe took the picture and turned from the pleading that was evident on John's face. *Not now*, she thought. That was close.

*   *   *

Strips of strapping tape were cut and wrapped on the outside of the container to both protect the artwork and its contents. The lid was wrapped three times just to make sure no one entered without a great deal of effort. And the final, completed project was placed in the living room, on top of the cabinet that contained the television. Temporarily, it held a distinguished and prominent place in the house, and all who entered would see it. Its final resting place in the hollowed basement of a forest home would have to wait as time was moving quickly and there was so much to do.

Chapter Eleven

The decision to spend their last evening together at Paul Bunyan Amusement Park was unanimous. Northern Minnesota is often called the home of Paul Bunyan, so the small amusement park in his honor had been a landmark for as long as Penelope, and even John, could remember.

An animated three-story-high lumberjack wearing a black-and-red plaid shirt with jeans and suspenders greeted the girls as they entered the park.

"Hello, Penelope from Ironwood and CeCe from Nebraska," boomed the well-known tall-tale hero.

Mirroring each other's reactions, the girls looked from Paul to each other and back to Paul again.

"How did he know my name?" murmured CeCe.

"I don't know, but I've heard that he knows all kids who enter the park. He greets everyone. He must have an informant somewhere." Penelope winked at John, who had sneaked in behind CeCe after conspiring with the clerk.

Penelope continued, "It's not a big amusement park, but it's fun and has some awesome rides. Plus, maybe

Dad will buy us a souvenir and some ice cream. I love chocolate ice cream in a waffle cone."

"Oh yeah, I love that too."

"Let's start at the Tilt-a-Whirl. I want to spin it as fast as possible," Penelope said. She thrust her arms outward and began to twirl her way down the path ahead of John and CeCe.

Watching her, both John and CeCe stopped to admire and smile at the joyous spirit they saw before themselves.

"I wish I had always known her," said CeCe without looking in John's direction.

"I love her too, CeCe, and you as well. And I wish more than anything that I could go back and make your wish come true. You two should have known each other from the very start." John let only his eyes slide toward CeCe in order to see her reaction to his comment. Physically, she didn't react, but her stinging words spoke volumes.

"You really messed this up," CeCe growled and ran to join her sister.

"I know," said John to himself.

*   *   *

Sitting in a large red car of the Tilt-a-Whirl, the girls pulled and gripped the circular wheel. Spinning faster created a force pushing them back in their seats. The riders' screams of dizzying joy erupted as the operator increased the speed. Faster. Faster. Faster. Spinning. Spinning.

To John it looked as if his daughters' heads could no longer be held up by their own necks. They were tilted in the direction of the moving ride. Watching as the ride came to a complete stop, he saw CeCe help Penelope out from the bar that had held them in place. They were holding hands as they came down the side stairs.

"Let's do it again! Come on, CeCe!"

"Are you okay?" John asked his youngest.

"Yeah, I am fine, Dad. I love it!"

"Are you okay?" John asked his oldest.

"I am absolutely fine," said CeCe. She raced around John to get back in line to repeat the process.

After four rounds of giggling on the Tilt-a-Whirl, the girls ran to the bumper cars.

The line for the bumper cars was always longest. People of all ages loved the jerking and smashing that took place under the musical canopy. Screams of surprise and maniacal laughter could be heard above the rock-and-roll beat.

When it was their turn, each chose from the remaining open cars in the back corner.

"Watch out, you two. I hope you're ready because here I come," said John. Leaning forward, he had a menacing grin.

"Ahhhh!" screamed Penelope as the cars disengaged from their off positions and drivers began in earnest to chase or evade each other.

Everyone was predator, and everyone became prey. When spotting someone they knew, recognition raised eyebrows, and smiles ensued. Backward and forward, steering wheels spinning—it was a rubberized demolition derby.

While the sisters chose to chase each other most often, at one point they both chose John as their victim.

"Watch out, Dad! Here we come!" said Penelope.

"Get him, sis!" responded CeCe.

John laughed and pretended to be offended then said, "Hey! What did I do? If you loved—"

He did not have time to complete his sentence. His girls hit him from the right side and front, which bumped his car back into another driver.

The girls laughed and stretched out high fives and took off after other unsuspecting victims.

The small family ran from the bumper cars to visit the Spooky House, which was not very spooky but fun anyway. Then it was on to the rock climbing wall. John cheered the girls higher, comforted by the straps and protective gear. Neither girl was bothered by heights and waved from their lofty positions at the top. Following the climb, the Ferris wheel became the next destination.

"Dad, you like the Ferris wheel. Come with us," pleaded Penelope.

"Yup, you know I do. I would be happy to join you two. None of that rocking-the-boat stuff though," laughed John. Crossing his eyes and tipping his head, he grabbed for both girls, who escaped his grasp and joined the short line waiting to board.

With Penelope in the middle, John's stomach remained calm as the three swayed their way to the highest point in the park and stopped.

"It is soooo pretty up here," said Penelope to no one in particular.

"Yeah, you can see so far," strained CeCe while turning her head in order to peek at the view behind their seat.

"Which way is our house, Dad?"

John pointed to the northwest, and all three turned to look toward that direction.

"Hmmm. I wish it would get a little darker. It would be so cool to see our stars from up here. It would be like we could reach out and touch them. I'll bet they are bigger and brighter from up here," said Penelope.

"That would be awesome," said CeCe. Tilting her head upward, she could imagine the picture that Penelope had created. With nothing but sky above, she knew that when she went home, she would be able to place this picture in her mind whenever she needed. In less than two weeks, many things had become important and would remind her of this place and these people. Forever. She knew she was taking them back with her whether she wanted to or not.

From out of the blue, CeCe surprised herself and blurted, "Why, John? Why didn't you call me? Or see me? Or contact me in some way? Why did you wait so long?"

Surprised by the outburst, John and Penelope snapped back to reality and turned toward CeCe.

"I honestly have no excuses, CeCe. At first, it was because I was mad at your mom. Then you moved, and I met Penelope's mother. I started a new life. I never for a moment forgot about you though. I always wondered and imagined, but I never did anything about it. Then when Anna died . . ." John paused for a moment to fight back the knot that was forming in his throat. "None of this was ever your fault. It was mine. I should have found a way. I should have . . ." John could no longer speak. Shaking his head back and forth, he closed his eyes. "I don't deserve your forgiveness, but maybe, just maybe, someday . . ." Again, he had to stop.

With nowhere to escape this private moment, Penelope was trapped. She tried to melt back into the seat. This was their discussion. She had settled her peace with CeCe and knew where she stood. Their future was secure. This was between her dad and her sister. She joined John with closed eyes. Her father had only cried twice before in her presence, and both times it had to do with her mother's death. Crying adults made her uneasy. It was too hard to see the two most important people in her life in such pain.

CeCe's hands were clenched white around the cool metal bar. "John, I—"

They were jerked back to reality as the Ferris wheel started its forward descent.

With Penelope in the middle, the family of three looked down toward the earth from which they came. No one said a word. No one dared to breathe. All emotions were right on the surface and created a tension that only needed the right straw to make it snap.

In unison, the three each gave a dazed thank-you to the attendant when he released them from their cage. The moment of honesty had passed, and everyone looked around for a distraction. John put his hands in his jean pockets and sneaked a slight, somewhat apologetic smile at his girls.

"Hey, I'm ready for ice cream. How about you two?" Penelope sensed she needed to save the moment, even the day, and food seemed to be their common ground.

Expelling pure relief, John responded, "Great idea, baby. Let's go."

The girls reverted to their previous gaiety now that they had a mission in mind. CeCe avoided John's eyes whenever possible.

Chocolate ice cream melted more than just heat from the day. It was obvious that no one was ready to head back to where they had been at the top of the Ferris wheel. This wasn't the time or place. There were too many people, too many teary emotions, and too much left to do.

Rushing frantically, they rotated through all the rides one more time.

"Well, are you girls done?" asked John.

"With the rides. But can we go to the gift shop? We have time," Penelope pleaded.

"All right, I'll give each of you five dollars. Buy what you want. Try to find a souvenir and not just candy."

"Thanks, Dad."

"Thanks, John." CeCe was careful not to touch John's hand as she took the offering. A glance at each other revealed the acknowledgment by both parties that their conversation would continue later.

The gift shop was typical of those found in most amusement parks: T-shirts, hats, candy, small toys of all types, pens, pencils, and even decks of cards. CeCe and Penelope wandered throughout the whole store, touching and examining all sorts of possibilities. Each girl chose a beautifully polished agate, a pen stamped with a picture of Paul Bunyan, and a small bear wearing a Paul Bunyan T-shirt. There was even enough money left for two tubes of honeysuckle-flavored honey.

*   *   *

"Did you have fun, girls?" John asked on the drive home. It was now past twilight.

Penelope mumbled behind her yawn, "It was great, Dad. Thanks so much for everything."

"Thanks. I had a nice time. And I love my souvenirs," CeCe added and then caught the yawn that Penelope had released.

Penelope leaned over and plopped her head on CeCe's shoulder. Squeezing the honey out of its clear tube, she swallowed the sweetness and spoke quietly,

"I wish you could see him like I see him. I'm going to miss you a lot."

"I will miss you a lot too," whispered CeCe. Laying her head against Penelope's, the sisters rode the rest of the way home without speaking. They were deep in thought, dreading the good-byes that would come the following day.

John caught a glimpse of his girls in the rearview mirror. His regrets concerning CeCe were like a heavy blanket placed on his heart. Its weight suppressed any true happiness. He knew his wrongdoings had altered all their lives. It was not fair to his daughters. They had no choice in any of this. Only the adults had the ability to make the necessary changes. CeCe's mother and John had known that things had to change before it was too late to repair the damage. John could only hope and pray.

*   *   *

"We are home, girls."

"I am so tired," said Penelope, trying to hide a huge yawn behind her hand.

"We should probably go to bed then," said CeCe. She gathered her belongings, looking at John as she spoke, and followed her family into the house. It was now or never. Tomorrow morning would be too busy to have the conversation that needed to happen. CeCe started chewing on her thumbnail as she entered the kitchen. Her stomach flipped and flopped like she was back on the Tilt-a-Whirl, and her mind was screaming at her to do it now. She repeated it over and over.

"I'll be right back. I forgot my bear and agate in the car," said Penelope. Not waiting for a response, she scooped up John's car keys from the kitchen table and let the screen door slam as she left to retrieve her valuables.

NOW! It had to be now.

"John?"

"CeCe?"

Father and daughter turned toward each other and smiled at the spontaneous mention of each other's name. Both let out a sigh and prepared themselves for what was to come. The time truly was now.

"Honey, please come and sit at the table with me."

CeCe nodded and did as she was asked, choosing the chair opposite John.

"CeCe, I cannot explain how and why I have made the choices I have. I've been wrong to keep you from Penelope, and I have been wrong to keep myself from you. I use to tell myself that I would call you maybe next week. Then next week would arrive, and I wouldn't call. That was happening week after week. I kept trying to convince myself that it would be fine if I waited just a bit longer. Then weeks turned into months, and by that time, I was afraid to call because it had been too long. I was, and am, ashamed of myself."

With her nose squished against the screen door, Penelope prepared herself for a loud "boo" in order to scare her dad and sister. But looking at them, she could see that whatever was happening didn't need interrupting. Her father had both of his hands on the table, with his palms facing upward. She couldn't see his face, but his voice was strained and intense, almost begging. And CeCe . . . well, she had her chin tucked into her chest. Her long hair was hanging over her right eye.

Sitting on the familiar top step, Penelope hugged her bear, clutched her rock, and chose not to disturb the moment. It was theirs and theirs alone.

John stopped. He didn't know what else to say. He would apologize every day for the rest of his life if he thought it would make things better. But for now, he would continue to try and explain. He couldn't stop trying—not now, not ever.

"I don't know how to make this right. The past cannot be erased, and I will forever regret my decisions." John stopped to clear his throat and wipe the freed tears off the side of his cheek. "All I can do is promise you that I will not let the past determine our future. What I mean is that I will call you. I will visit you. I will have you visit me here. I will never let anything happen to the relationship you have with Penelope. I will never leave you again."

Penelope stood up from her perch on the step and prepared herself to speak to John and CeCe if needed. She knew that they had to be brought together. They had to start over and learn to forgive. *One more minute,* she thought, *just one more minute.* Then she saw CeCe lift her head. Her eyes were locked on those across from her. Penelope held her breath and watched.

Blinking slowly, CeCe stood, walked around the table, and chose to hug her father for the first time. Thin arms embraced John's shoulders, as hands clutched the back of his denim shirt.

John folded CeCe into his arms and let her face burrow into his neck. Years of longing and relief washed over him as he closed his eyes. Trembling, he rested his cheek on the top of CeCe's head and inhaled.

Both cried softly and let tears release the hurt that for years had been held inside their hearts.

Tears didn't need to be coaxed from the spectator looking in at the scene on the other side of the screen. She too felt shaky for all the same reasons as those at the kitchen table. It really wouldn't matter what they said or did next. She knew the healing had begun. Quietly, without interrupting the magic before her, Penelope entered and slowly climbed the stairs to her bedroom, a wide smile spreading across her face.

*   *   *

Assuming her sister asleep, CeCe tiptoed around the bedroom she would now forever share with her sister; she got ready for bed.

"Hey, you," whispered Penelope.

"Wha? What are you doing up? I thought you were sleeping. You scared me half to death."

"I couldn't go to sleep without making one more memory before tomorrow," said Penelope. The grin on her face didn't hide the sadness that had formed around her green eyes.

Climbing into the now familiar sheets, CeCe spoke first, "John and I are going to try this father-and-daughter thing. I am tired of fighting it, and I really want to see what it is like having a dad, having a dad like you have a dad. He seems to be trying and has been patient and honest with me. At this point, I cannot forget, but maybe I can forgive. So I am going to see how it goes. No promises, but I thought you should know. That means I will be back." This time it was CeCe's turn to flash a brilliant smile.

"Yes! I knew it! I knew it! Yes! When are you coming back? Is it soon? Are you all right? Should we write to each other too?" Penelope kept the questions rolling without waiting for answers. Penelope stopped. "Right now. This moment is the best ever, CeCe. Right now. We are sisters forever. I love you."

"I love you more," CeCe said, hugging her baby sister.

Chapter Twelve

"Are you sure you have everything?" asked Penelope, taking one last look under the bed.

"I think so," said CeCe. "I can always get anything I forget next time."

Both girls stopped, smiled the same smile, and continued their search for lonely socks, missing jewelry, and anything else that may have found its way to the floor.

CeCe smashed her belongings into a small black suitcase. "Hey, I should try zipping it. It looks kind of full."

"I'll help," said Penelope.

Although it took the two of them pushing and squeezing items back inside before the zipper safely sealed all valuables, the task was now complete.

CeCe also had a backpack ready for the bus ride, complete with a book, a journal for writing, a special rock to make her smile, and a framed picture to comfort and remind her of the rest of her family.

"Here is a bag with some munchies for the trip. I packed a couple of our cookies and some candy from the treat drawer. There are a couple of sandwiches downstairs. Don't forget them. Is there anything else you might need?" asked Penelope.

"No, I'm fine. I'm sure I have plenty. I will carry the suitcase down if you carry my backpack."

"Sure," said Penelope, "should we have Dad come up and get the suitcase?"

"Did I hear my name? What do you need from me?" said Dad, standing in the doorway. His arms were crossed over his denim shirt, and the sleeves folded to a three-quarter length that revealed his silver Timex. Rolling his arm to check the time, John said, "Let's go, girls. We don't want to be late. I'll get the suitcase. Do you have everything?"

Looking into her father's eyes, CeCe said, "I think so. I didn't realize that I had so much and that I had it all over this room."

"I wouldn't have noticed. Your sister has a habit of carpeting the floor with her clothes and books and papers and anything else that can be dropped and forgotten."

"Hey, I clean it sometimes. It was sparkling before CeCe got here—well, for a minute or two."

The new family of three laughed a nervous laugh. No one was talking about the moment of good-bye that was yet to come. No one wanted to talk about how wonderful and scary this trial run had been. No one wanted to waste time thinking about how quickly this visit had passed.

"Let's go then," said John. He hugged both girls at once. With a squeeze, he released them, grabbed the suitcase, and headed toward the stairs.

On the top step, CeCe paused. "You two go ahead, I think I forgot something."

"We will meet you downstairs," said Penelope.

Walking back into the bedroom she had shared with her sister, CeCe looked around one last time. So much had happened, yet there was still so much to do.

Taking a pencil from her backpack, CeCe added an additional line to the almost completed *Fun Things to Do* list: Let's do it all again, next time!

*   *   *

The Greyhound Bus Depot in Ironwood was a small gas station with an attached diner. Regular coffee drinkers, seated at the counter, were discussing the recent heat wave while a woman in a short pink apron refilled the coffee cups of a couple seated at a corner booth.

"We are a bit early. Would you girls like something to eat or drink?" asked John. The three seated themselves at a window booth, with the girls seated together opposite their father.

"Yeah, can we share a malt?" asked Penelope, giving her sister a quick jab of her elbow into her side.

"Uh. Oh, yeah. That would be great," smiled CeCe.

"Sure," said John. "Can you two agree on one flavor?"

"What is your favorite? I love chocolate with anything. They always put whipping cream and a cherry on top."

"Chocolate is perfect. Can we add a banana to it?" asked CeCe.

"What can I get for you today?" asked the waitress holding her order pad, ready to write.

"Well, these lovely girls will split a chocolate-banana malt, and I will have a cup of coffee. Thanks," said John. "Oh, and make sure there are two cherries with lots of whipped cream."

"Got it," winked the waitress.

Everyone at the table pretended to be busy by skimming the menu, watching traffic out the window, or appearing to be interested in the café's clientele. No one was speaking.

The arrival of their order gave conversation choices.

"Mmmm, this cherry is just perfect," said Penelope, pulling the stem from between her front teeth.

"So good," murmured CeCe.

John picked up his coffee cup, inhaled deeply, and held the cup with both hands wrapped around it as if freezing and trying to warm them.

Each girl took turns using their long-handled silver spoons to scoop out chunks of banana wrapped in creamy chocolate ice cream. Their politeness was genuine, and it was the type afforded sisters who were no longer strangers.

With about half of the malt left, John put his cup down. "The bus is here, girls. Time to go."

Mouths froze in mid bite. It seemed an eternity, but Penelope broke the stillness by placing her spoon into the tall malt glass. CeCe followed her sister's lead. All three slid from their curved booth seats and walked in silence to the cash register.

"How was everything?" asked the waitress.

"Everything was wonderful," said John. Looking down at his girls, he smiled and handed a five dollar bill to the waitress. He turned toward the door holding his daughter's suitcase and didn't wait for cash back.

Penelope reached for CeCe's hand and squeezed. They walked behind their father, side by side, hand in hand, and matched their father's footsteps.

A teenage girl and the bus driver were standing outside the door of the bus. She handed her ticket to the driver, laughed, and climbed the steps that led to the interior. Her suitcase had already been loaded in the cargo hold.

John handed CeCe's suitcase to the bus driver and said something to the driver that neither girl could hear. They watched the manly handshake and assumed all was right. With resignation, John turned to see two young girls holding hands and looking at him. Their eyes were pleading with him to say the right things, to do whatever would make this moment less painful and sad.

"Girls, it is time for CeCe to go home to her mother. Do you have your ticket, honey?"

CeCe pulled the ticket from the side pouch of her backpack and handed it to John. She didn't trust her voice to say even one word. She wanted to see her mom. She didn't want to leave. She knew she would be back, but the leaving was never going to be easy. In fact, she was pretty sure this was the first of many sad good-byes. However, on the flip side of that thinking, there would also be many opportunities for hello.

John handed the ticket to the driver.

"Young lady, come on aboard," he said.

Rubbing his hands, John knelt down on one knee in front of CeCe. He took her hands in his and looked directly into her brown eyes. "Honey, I cannot tell you how happy I am that you agreed to come here, that you had the courage to come all this way to meet people you didn't even know. I am proud of you, and I am proud to be your father. You are smart, beautiful, and kind. I vow to keep the promises I made to you last night. I will see you again, and I will call all the time. I love you, CeCe." John embraced his daughter in a bear hug, and for the second time in less than twenty-four hours, she hugged her father.

CeCe pulled away first and wiped away the now steady flow of tears and turned toward her sister.

The usually talkative and smiling Penelope was wide-eyed, breathing hard, and holding her mouth tight.

CeCe wrapped her arms around her little sister without waiting for words as Penelope's reached for CeCe. Stroking her sister's hair, CeCe was the first to speak.

"I love you, Penelope. I will be back. I promise. I will call you, and I promise to write every day."

Finding her voice, Penelope said through her own stream of tears, "I love you too. I will miss you so much. You are the best sister ever."

CeCe placed her foot on the first step and turned back for one more look at her family.

"Goodbye, Penelope. Goodbye, Dad."

"I love you, honey. Call when you get home."

"See you later, CeCe. I love you!"

Choosing a window seat, CeCe waved to her family as the bus pulled away and continued to wave until she could no longer see her dad and her sister.

John and Penelope waved until the bus was no longer in sight.